ZOMBIE
18

Alan Cowsill

BULLPEN
PRODUCTIONS

About the Author

Alan Cowsill has worked as a writer and editor for Marvel UK/Panini and Eaglemoss Publishing. He created the award-winning *Classic Marvel Figurine Collection* and *DC Super Hero Collection* and worked on the *Marvel Chess Collection* and *Marvel Movie Collection*. His books include *Colin the Goblin, Stormwatcher, DC Comics: A Year by Year Visual Chronicle, Marvel Comics: 75 Years of Comic Art, Spider-Man Chronicle, Marvel Avengers Character Encyclopedia* and the award-winning graphic novel *World War One* (Campfire). He was also one of the writers of *Revolutionary War* for Marvel. He is presently the Managing Director of Bullpen Productions.

For updates, behind-the-scenes secrets of *Zombie 18* and more join the mailing list. Email: "Z18 Mailing List" to alancowsill@ gmail.com

We need your help too. If you enjoyed this book please leave a quick review on Amazon or whichever platform or online store you bought it from.

Published by Bullpen Productions

Copyright © 2017 Alan Cowsill

Contact: alancowsill@gmail.com

Website: www.alancowsill.com

www.bullpenproductions.co.uk

ISBN: 978-0-9956994-1-0

Cover artwork:
Lalit Kumar Sharma (Pencils/inks)
Alan Craddock (Colour)

ONE

I will not die.

I know it's going to happen. I know it's going to happen real soon, but I'm going to fight it.

I am going to STAY in control. I am NOT going to lose it. I am NOT going to die.

Who am I trying to kid?

Jack died. My folks died. Just about everyone I've ever known's died. And I'll die. That's why I'm doing this. Why I'm writing this down in one last mad crazy rush before it happens.

Before I become one of them.

Maybe it'll help me hold on to things. Or at the very least let you know what happened to us all.

Maybe it'll even help you.

I don't really care. I'm here and I'm about to die and I need to do something so my last few hours aren't spent screaming and crying and…

My name's Alex Stevens and I'm seventeen years old.

Tomorrow's my birthday.

Tomorrow I'm eighteen.

And that's why I'm going to die.

I know the old world wasn't perfect, but these days it seems that way. It really does.

It's less than three months since the Change and I miss so much. So many things. So many people.

Still, at least I made it to London. I always wanted to come down here. Used to think I'd live down here when I was older.

Older.

That's a laugh. Today I'm about as old as you can get.

I arrived here at first light after taking the walk yesterday. Didn't take me long to find this place. One thing about what's happened, there's plenty of decent accommodation available if you can put up with the neighbours. I can hear them groaning and shambling about down below. Thought I saw some kids in what's left of Parliament earlier but I stayed clear. I've left people behind me. I don't want to do a Jack and try to kill them. That would be most uncool. Not to mention wrong.

So here I am. Top-floor penthouse and what a view! I'm sitting on the balcony as I scrawl these words, looking out over what's left of London. Big Ben's just across the river. It's seen better days. There's still smoke coming out of a hole in the clock face on the south side. The Houses of Parliament seem to have got off lightly. It's clearly seen better days but at least it's still there. The other buildings lining the Thames are pretty much burnt-out shells. In the distance, way over the city, a few buildings and tower blocks are still burning. The Shard's gone, snapped in half. What's left of it a jagged needle on the horizon. All the cities burned after the Change. Guess they didn't have much choice. All that gas and electric running wild. All the dropped cigs and left-on cookers.

Boom!

To the right, I can see St. Paul's Cathedral and it still looks amazing. Okay, so there's a massive hole in the roof, but the cathedral is still there watching over the Thames. Which is more than can be said for the Pineapple or Gherkin or whatever it was called. Nothing left of that at all.

Listen, sorry if I'm rambling, but this is more for me than you. I'm also trying to work out where to start from. I mean, obviously, here and now. With me overlooking London's destroyed skyline, the sun rising, a few corpses staggering around aimlessly below. The London Eye's still there. It's stopped turning, but the pods are filled with people who were trapped inside when the Change occurred. They're dead, but that doesn't stop them moving. Being dead doesn't stop most people moving these days. At least if you're over eighteen. The living dead will be trapped in those small glass pods until the whole thing eventually topples over into the Thames, or they stop being zombies. Still, at least they have a nice view. Other zombies are occasionally queuing up at the foot of it. How weird is that? They should get a life.

Sorry, that probably wasn't funny.

I can also see Charing Cross station and the dead are there too. A few trains crashed and burned. The hotel above the station pretty much collapsed in on itself. Must've been one hell of a blaze. A couple of trains are jutting out of the wreckage, melted and charred from the heat. One train's hanging off the bridge leading into the station, almost as if it's trying to decide whether to take the plunge into the dark water below. There are a few corpses standing on what's left of the platforms. They shuffle about, chasing the odd pigeon or fighting over some scrap of meat they've found. They seem to be waiting for trains that will never arrive.

Anyway, I've got to start before, that much is obvious. Not too far before though. I mean, you don't really need to know about the time I cut my leg open playing football in the back garden and had to have stitches. Or how I used to stay up late watching horror movies with my dad. My mum used to say they'd give me nightmares but Dad said they'd be good for me. Guess he was right about that one. These days I think of those movies as basic training. No, you don't need to know about that, but you do need to know about Jack's birthday and maybe just before that.

When we first met the girls.

Yeah, let's start with the girls. Kim, Molly and Cara.

Meeting them saved our lives.

We were staying at a Retreat in Ilkley. It was a school trip to mellow a few of us out before the exams and a vague attempt to make us feel more religious at Easter – after all, the Retreat was run by monks. There were thirty of us on the trip. Four from each year plus five teachers to make sure we didn't get into trouble – or in Kegs' case more trouble than usual. Our school, Campion, was in St. Helens, a small town about ten miles from Liverpool. It's not a bad school and it's not a good school. Actually now it's a burnt-out wreck of a school filled with the living dead, but you know what I mean. I was in the sixth form, not much time left at the place. A prized position at Huddersfield University waiting for me providing I got the right grades. (A and two Bs, in case you're wondering. Exams cancelled due to apocalypse.) The trip was only for a few days. A look at York and a life-affirming walk on the moors that sucked big time. It was raining and the moors were all kinds of boring. The highlight was Mr Lee getting shouted out by a couple of Rangers for taking kids out on the moors when the weather was so bad. He got us lost and we all got soaked.

That's when we met the girls. Not out on the moors but on the way back to Ilkley. We'd pulled into a service station to get some petrol. I was in the newsagents hoping to find a decent book to read when Jack and Matt came rushing up to me as if their lives depended on it.

"Reckon he'll be able to handle the mission?" Jack smirked.

"Think so," Matt grinned. "And let's face it, the only other option is Kegs."

All three of us looked across the shop, to where Kegs was busy picking on a couple of kids from Year Eight, smacking one over the head with a comic. Kegs was something of a throwback to prehistoric times and the worst bully in the history of the school. It was an all-boys school, by the way. Which explains why I was hopeless at talking to girls and totally terrified when Jack grinned and said, "Come with us, we've found you a girlfriend."

I knew Matt and Jack pretty well and was friends with Johnny, Matt's younger brother. They were like a school double act and could get away with murder – mainly because everyone liked them. Matt was captain of the rugby team, while Jack liked cricket. Actually he was obsessed with cricket and was the only person I've ever met who could do a googly and actually knew what 'silly mid-off' meant. Think Jack saw sport as another way of impressing girls (which was his favourite hobby) while Matt saw sport as a way of helping him get into the RAF. That was his main ambition and probably what made him slightly more human than a lot of the other rugby players at the school – who tended to be more like Kegs in their outlook and attitude. Matt's brother Johnny should have been on the school trip with us, but had got in trouble at cadets the week before and was staying back home as some kind of punishment duty. All part of the fun when your father runs the local squadron.

Anyway, the girls. When Jack mentioned them, I was terrified.

"Er, I just want to get a book," I mumbled, hating the fact that I was blushing at the thought of talking to girls. I was seventeen, it was ridiculous. I'd have to start talking to them sometime. It was just that, right there and then, tomorrow seemed a much better time to start.

Before I knew what was happening they'd almost dragged me out of the newsagents to the entrance to the food court, where six schoolgirls were chatting and giggling to each other.

They were all about our age and in school uniforms far smarter than ours. Not that we had ours on. We were in our trekking gear, which in my case made me feel even more stupid.

"Which one do you fancy?" Jack whispered, adding seriously, "I bagsy the one with the bob though. She's lovely."

I mumbled something lame and suddenly found myself facing the girls with absolutely nothing cool or interesting to say. Not that it seemed to be damaging Jack's chances. Don't know how he did it, but within a few seconds of flashing his smile and making them laugh, he'd peeled the girl with the bob from her friends and led her away from everyone.

"Cara, what are you like!" one of her friends laughed.

For his part, Matt seemed glad the major competition had gone and was almost holding court, the girls eating up his every word.

"Kegs alert," I whispered.

"Alright girls, who wants me?" Kegs said, a little too loudly for his own good.

"So, anyway, this glider…?" a girl called Molly asked, ignoring Kegs completely.

"It was pretty amazing," Matt smiled. "Just me and the pilot miles above the countryside. They let me fly at one point too."

"Are you a cadet as well?" another girl smiled.

"No," I replied, feeling incredibly stupid. "I got a new bike a few weeks ago though."

"Really, what kind? My boyfriend's got a Harley."

"Err, not a motorbike," I mumbled, deciding to stare at my feet for a few years. "Just a bicycle. Good one though."

"Oh," the girl said, sounding a little disappointed. "Never mind, maybe you'll get one when you're older. When I'm on the back of my boyfriend's Harley, it's, like, so totally awesome."

"Don't listen to Denise," a new girl said, joining her friends. "One, it wasn't a Harley, just some cheap second-hand rust bucket, and two, it wasn't her boyfriend, just some dodgy biker who fancied his chances."

Denise made a strange sound and started to blush herself.

I looked up and was pretty much stunned.

Kimberly Davis. It was a little like being struck by lightning. Kim looked more like twenty than seventeen and was a little shorter than me, with deep brown eyes and long jet-black hair curling around her shoulders. She was the most beautiful thing I've ever seen. Swear to God.

"Dude, you're staring," Matt whispered, laughing and then adding, "Can't blame you though. She's a babe."

"I'm Kim," she smiled. "So, do you come here often?"

Matt laughed out loud at this and started chatting away to her. For my part, I couldn't talk. My palms were suddenly even sweatier and my stomach had gone AWOL.

It turned out they were on the way back to their private school from a hockey tournament.

"What school?" Matt asked.

"St. Mary's," Denise said.

"Excuse me, I think you'll find it's actually St. Mary's School for Girls," Kim smiled, putting on a posh accent and then adding in her normal voice, "At least, that's what they tell our folks when they fleece them for the fees every term. Not that my parents are bothered. They're too busy travelling around the world to care what happens to me and Lizzie."

We both looked at her expectantly. Kegs too, who'd been strangely quiet since Kim's arrival. Judging by the look on his face (and I know this from talking about it later) he was a little bit in love with her himself.

"My sister," she said. "The one playing the really violent games in the arcade. Don't think they've managed to refine her that much yet. Thankfully."

We both glanced at the arcade, where an innocent-looking twelve-year-old was blowing monsters away on some computer game. A young kid from our school called Billy was watching her, totally smitten.

"What do you think you're doing?" a stern woman's voice said from nearby.

Kim flinched a little as one of her teachers walked out of the toilet – and straight into Jack and Cara, who were kissing like their lives depended on it.

"I said what are you doing?" she repeated, her voice making ice appear around her.

"Biology 101?" Cara smiled, still holding a slightly nervous-looking Jack by the hand.

"Coach, now," the teacher ordered.

"Looks like it's time to go," Kim smiled, moving away. "After all, they don't want you corrupting us sweet innocent girls."

We both laughed at this, and I've got to admit I felt a little lost when they left. The world was suddenly a little less colourful.

"See, it wasn't that bad," Matt grinned. "And I think Kim's mate fancied you."

"Yeah, well, that's that," I half-smiled, irritated by Matt's words. "I mean, it's not like we're going to see them again."

"Result," Jack grinned, rejoining us and holding on to his mobile like it was a prize. "Not only did I get a snog, but I got her number as well. She's going to sneak out to meet me later. Looks like I'm going to have a birthday to remember after all!"

It was dusk by the time we got back to the Retreat, which was on the edge of the moors. Originally a huge Victorian mansion, the main building had been converted into the Retreat about fifty years before. Half of it was purely for the monks and half for visitors. I'd imagine it was quite a creepy place at the best of times, but when darkness fell, the shadows and silence made it really sinister. The cold and barren moors overlooking it only added to the feeling of gloomy isolation. A winding and narrow driveway led from the road to the main building and there was a converted gatehouse near the entrance where the caretaker and his wife lived. Once inside the Retreat's huge double doors, there was a library and dining room to the right and the chapel and monks' quarters to the left. No TV or radio in the whole building. According to legend, the bedrooms were haunted by a kid who'd died there a century before. A few of the guys had been out ghost-hunting the night before but, oddly enough, had not found anything.

I mean, life after death. What a stupid idea.

One of the younger kids, Jeff Holt (twelve years old, nervous and stuttered), had been pretty spooked by the whole thing and gone in to sleep with his brother Pete (sixteen, good runner). But again, I'm going off on a sidetrack. I mean, you need to know who these kids are. Some are important to what happens next. But I really should get to the meat of it. Mr Lee would mark me down on that, if he wasn't dead.

Most of our free time at the Retreat was spent in the library. It was really just a pretty big lounge with a few chairs and a table in. There was also a huge bookcase filled with all sorts of books. Cheap paperbacks left by previous guests through to old encyclopaedias and biographies. Some were over a hundred years old. And yes, I'm a reader. I love books. Always have. Anyway, it was either reading books, playing games on your mobile (unless one of the teachers caught you and confiscated it – probably to play with themselves as they seemed equally bored) or flick football with spare change on the dining table.

Yup, things really were that boring.

These days I'd kill for boring.

"Hey, Alex, over here. Can you help me with my revision?" Matt said, winking as he did so.

He was standing by Pete's side, both looking at something on the younger kid's laptop. Mr Green, the only teacher in the room with us, was dozing in an old armchair in front of the fire, a newspaper spread out on his chest.

"Managed to get online at last," Pete whispered. "Got someone who wants to talk to you."

I smiled at the face on the laptop. It was Matt's brother, Johnny.

"Good holiday?" he grinned.

"Amazing," I smiled back, looking into the small camera built into the laptop. "Non-stop fun. How about you?"

"Great," he lied. "Dad's got me washing dishes at this meal for all the officers. Some of the cadets are waiting on them hand and foot."

"Well, you did yell at Dad in front of the whole squad," Matt said at my side. "Wasn't terribly bright considering he's in charge of the place. How's sis?"

"Fine," Johnny answered. "Her and a few mates are having a sleepover. The house is full of screaming nine-year-old girls –

think I'd rather stay here and do the dishes."

I smiled. My own sister, Gabs, had been looking forward to going over to Johnny's house all week. Helen, his sister, was one of her close friends, but I think the real reason she was looking forward to it was the fact that she had a massive crush on Johnny. Something I liked teasing her about at every opportunity.

"Better go," Johnny said. "Dad doesn't know I snuck the laptop into the kitchen with me. Thinks I'm hard at work. Better show willing. Maybe he'll let me join you tomorrow or something, you never know. See ya."

We said our farewells and the screen went blank.

"My dad still thinks that sort of thing's like something from a sci-fi movie," Pete grinned.

"Shame Johnny couldn't make it out here, though."

Matt seemed a little quiet about something.

"What?" I asked.

"Nothing," he replied. "Just that him and Dad haven't been getting on lately. We both know he doesn't want to be a cadet anymore, but he's not got around to telling Dad."

"Well, that's understandable," I smiled. "Your dad is a little scary."

Matt nodded and directed my attention to Jack. I think it was more to change the subject than anything.

Jack was sitting in a chair, texting Cara. They'd been sending each other messages from the moment they'd parted.

"Must be love," Matt sang jokingly, only to have Jack throw a cushion at him.

The noise seemed to bring Mr Green out of his slumber. Or maybe it was the smell of food coming in from the kitchen.

"Almost feeding time," the teacher said. "You lot set the table, I'll go and see when it'll be ready. Try not to kill anyone while I'm out of the room. That does mean you, Fitzpatrick."

Kegs tried his best to look innocent but failed. The little kid he'd been approaching scurried away, looking relieved.

Just after Green left the room, Jack glanced down at his phone before standing up and moving towards the window.

"What is it with this place?" he said, more to himself than anyone else. "Been a bad signal all day – and now I can't even get one."

"Probably the ghosts," I joked.

"You might be right," he smiled, pressing redial.

"You okay?" I asked.

"Just a little tired. Must be all the excitement."

I nodded, but wasn't convinced. He suddenly looked very pale, as though he might be coming down with flu.

"Now that Alex has mentioned it, you don't look that good," Matt teased. "In fact, if you want, I'll meet Cara later. Just to help you out, like."

"You wish," he coughed, slurring his words slightly as though he was drunk. "Weird. My arm's all stiff. Like…"

Jack's words caught in his throat. He made a soft rasping sound and collapsed. Matt was by his side in an instant.

"Jack, it's not funny," Matt said.

It was clear that Jack wasn't messing around. His face had gone pale, as though all the blood had left it. At the time I thought it was just my imagination, but the skin seemed to be getting tighter, like his flesh was starting to rot before our very eyes. Within seconds, his skin was grey and lifeless.

Everything was unreal. I'd heard people say that when bad things happen it seems like you're watching it from a distance. That was how I felt. All my senses seemed to have gone into overdrive.

"He's not breathing," Matt said, checking again for a pulse as his first-aid training kicked in. "Someone call an ambulance. Alex, get a teacher in here now. Tell them what's happened."

"Be careful," Kegs said. "It might be some contagious disease."

"He's my friend!" Matt cried out. "Just phone for some help."

"I'm trying," I heard Kegs answer, as I rushed out the door. "Line's engaged."

As I reached the door, Matt was starting to pound at Jack's heart, performing CPR, trying in vain to get our friend to breathe.

My mind was racing as I burst into the kitchen.

"Sir, we need help," I shouted, tripping over something lying just inside the door. I landed on the cold kitchen floor with a nasty smack. Shaken by the fall, it took me a few seconds to make out what had tripped me up.

Mr Green.

I was staring at his dead face. His blank, lifeless eyes staring straight into my own.

"Sir?" I said, moving towards him.

I was more than scared now. More than terrified. I touched Mr Green's shoulder.

Nothing.

"Sir, come on. Wake up. We need help!" I yelled, turning him onto his back and shaking his shoulders. His body was limp and lifeless. I let go, the corpse making a dull thud as it hit the floor.

And then I saw them and started to realise just how bad things were.

Four more bodies were in the kitchen.

Three cooks and a monk. Two were slumped over the cooking area and looked like they'd passed out while chopping onions for the food. The third was at the massive cast-iron stove. It was then I smelt the gas from the cooker and noticed a pan containing stew had been spilt over the cooker, knocking out the flame. I rushed over and turned the hob off, holding my breath as I opened the windows and back door.

Had they been gassed?

I ran back out of the kitchen, pushing the door open and dragging Mr Green's body out. I was about to get help from my mates when I noticed another body at the foot of the staircase. Another monk. I checked for breath but there was none. The flesh was stone cold and the skin seemed to be tightening over the body before my eyes – as though weeks of decay were taking place in a few minutes.

I looked up the stairs and made a decision, bounding up them two at a time. Another monk was lying motionless at the top.

I opened the first door I came to – it was Mr Lee's room – and saw the teacher and Mrs Jones lying next to each other on the bed, arms enfolded. For a second I breathed a sigh of relief; they looked calm and asleep. I think I even smiled. The rumours about their affair were true, then.

"Sir, we need help," I said. "Something bad's happening."

No answer.

The panic started to return.

When I flicked on the light, I could see their bodies were

already taking on a deathly pallor. The cheeks were sallow. Again, it looked like they'd been dead for weeks rather than minutes.

I fled the room for the next one. Another teacher, Mr Lennon, was slumped in an armchair.

"What's happening?" I mumbled, unable to really comprehend what I was witnessing.

I'd liked Mr Lennon. He taught history and was cool and had a way of making the lessons seem fun. For a second I couldn't move or breathe. It was all just too strange, too far removed from anything I'd ever experienced. I rushed to the sink in the corner of the small, dark bedroom and was sick. Looking up at my reflection in the mirror I noticed I was nearly as pale as the dead around me. I washed my face and dried my hands on a towel, leaving the room in a daze to check the others. Most were empty but two contained corpses. A priest who'd died while praying and a monk lying near his bed.

"This isn't right," I mumbled to myself.

Looking back, it amazes me how close to death I was.

By the time I got back to the main room and my friends, the panic was spreading. Matt was crying and screaming, still doing CPR on Jack, who was staring blankly back, his own lips and face grey. Some of the skin even seemed to be peeling from his lips like it was rotting. A few of the Year Sevens were whimpering softly to themselves.

"I think he's dead," Matt said. "I don't know what else we can do. It just doesn't make sense. People just don't die like that."

"Apparently they do," I whispered.

Matt looked at me, confused. A huge explosion was heard from outside. So loud it made the windows shake. Despite everything, a few kids ran to the window to see what had happened.

"Something's on fire," one of them said. "Down in the town. Looks really serious."

"What do you mean?" Matt asked me.

"They're all dead," I explained, feeling as though I was watching everything from a great distance. "All of them. The teachers, the monks. They're dead."

"They can't be," Matt said.

"Take a look if you don't believe me. They're just lying there like Jack."

"Maybe we should open the windows," Pete, who was in Year Ten, suggested. "Maybe there's a gas leak or something."

"They're locked," Pete answered.

"Get them open," Matt said to Kegs. "I'll check the others."

Kegs picked up a chair and hurled it against the window, the sound of the smashing glass making us all jump.

I caught sight of Matt leaving the room and was annoyed that he didn't believe me.

There was only silence outside. No cars, no shouts, nothing. Complete and utter silence.

It was like God had pressed pause on the whole world.

And then it all changed.

"He's alive!" Stu Masters shouted. "Jack's alive!"

Everyone turned to look at Jack.

Stu was half right.

Jack was moving.

He just wasn't alive.

TWO

Funny thing is, for a second or two, I felt happy. We all did. Jack was alive!

One look at him told me something wasn't right. That the thing staggering to its feet might have looked like Jack – albeit in a blue-hey-is-that-rigor-mortis-setting-in-already kind of way – but the face told the truth. Jack had left the building.

Unfortunately Stu got a little too close.

"Jack, you worried us," he said, moving to Jack's side to help him.

It happened quickly. Too quickly. Jack's dead hand snapped out and grabbed Stu by the neck.

There was a sickening crack and Stu's body went limp.

For a few seconds none of us could move. It was wrong. None of us could deal with it.

"Hey, what have you done?" a friend of Stu's shouted, rushing forwards.

Jack's arm lashed out, sending the kid flying head first against the wall. He didn't move. There was no need to check if he was okay. The twisted shape of his body and the sheer force of the impact told us he wasn't.

The only sound came from the thing that had once been our

friend. It was the sound of Death breathing.

A young kid started to cry. Jack lurched menacingly towards him. I'd like to say I jumped in and saved the day, but I didn't. I was far too scared and way too freaked out to move. Some part of my brain was trying to convince me it was all a bad dream but I knew it wasn't. It was real and it would soon get far worse.

Someone screamed from upstairs.

"Matt," I whispered, snapping out of my horrified trance.

"Jack, what's going on mate?" a kid asked, stepping in between Jack and the Year Seven boy.

Jack's only response was more of the awful, deathly breathing.

"He's a zombie," Kegs said. "He's a zombie and he's going to eat us all."

I was halfway to the door to check on Matt when I saw Kegs pick up a chair and smash it over the back of Jack's head.

It should have hurt Jack. In fact, it should have killed him. Instead, it did nothing. Actually that's not true – it bent his head out of shape. Think the impact might have even snapped Jack's neck. Not that it seemed to bother Jack. He continued to shamble forward, his head now tilted at a totally unnatural angle.

"What are you doing?" a kid called Doug shouted. "You've killed him!"

"How can I kill him?" Kegs said, already looking around the room for another potential weapon. "He's already dead."

"Help!" Matt cried out again.

I opened the door and rushed out, just in time to see a beaten and bloody Matt collapse down the staircase. At the top of the stairs, Mr Lee and the monk I'd passed only minutes before were watching it all with dead eyes. Their flesh was now even more rotted. Bits of bone could be seen pushing through Mr Lee's jaw.

"Matt, you okay?" I asked, rushing to his side.

I flinched when I saw his left leg. It was broken and Matt was pale. A haunted, crazy expression in his eyes.

"He tried to kill me," he whispered. "I was just trying to wake him up when his arms came out and he... he tried to strangle me. Not just him. The others too. They've all gone insane."

"Not insane," I said. "I think they're dead."

Mr Lee was looking at the stairs as though he'd never seen them before. I screamed as the monk stepped forward and tumbled past us both. It landed with a terrible sound of breaking bone. I couldn't tear my gaze away as I realised it was still somehow alive (or at least moving... are zombies really alive? Jury's still out on that one. Ask me again tomorrow). It was twisted out of shape but its one good arm was outstretched and dragging the rest of its mangled body towards us. Above us, Mr Lee had worked out how to deal with the stairs and was starting to stagger down them.

"Think your leg's broken, but we've got to move anyway," I said.

"You think?" Matt replied, half laughing.

Mrs Jones (she wasn't that good-looking anymore) and some more monks were starting to follow Mr Lee down the staircase.

"Come on, let's do it," I said, wrapping an arm around Matt, trying my best to protect his twisted leg.

He screamed with pain and I stopped.

"Go," he said, under panting heavy breaths. "I can do it. Only a few yards."

I could hear the monk dragging his broken body after us, the heavy footsteps of the others stumbling their way down the staircase. As I opened the door, I risked a glance back. Mr Lee and another monk were at the bottom of the staircase now and the broken monk was dragging himself towards us. For the first time I saw their eyes. They weren't blank and lifeless anymore. They were burning red, filled with pain and anger and hatred.

I slammed the door closed and let Matt collapse against it. As he slid down to the floor, he let out a cry of pain. Another kid – Bobby Hargraves, thirteen, played the flute – was lying dead at Jack's feet. Kegs was pushing Jack towards the window using a chair like some lunatic lion tamer. The door behind me pushed forward suddenly. Matt screamed as a dead hand grabbed his shoulder.

"Help!" I cried, but no one looked over; they were too busy being terrified by Jack. Doug moved to his feet and rushed to Kegs' side, whispering something into Kegs' ear. Without warning, Kegs dropped the chair and together they rushed Jack, pushing him towards the smashed window. Jack staggered back, taken by surprise, and was flipped out of the broken window. He rolled down the grass to the driveway.

"Over here!" I yelled, just as the door was pushed open wide enough for Mr Lee to stagger into the room. One of the monks was behind him but I managed to slam the door closed before he could follow the teacher through the narrow gap.

"Are you okay, sir?" a Year Eight asked.

"Keep away!" I warned, but it was too late. Mr Lee's arms shot down and started to strangle the young kid (Billy Drake, twelve, liked football and collected teddy bears but that was a secret).

"Kegs!" I shouted. "Over here. Keep the door shut, they're trying to get in!"

For once Kegs did what I asked, pressing his back against the door. The sound of hands and fists could be heard thumping against the other side of the wood.

"Let him go," Doug said, approaching the teacher. Or what had once been our teacher.

I looked on in horror as Mr Lee kept one hand on Billy's throat and slapped Doug away with the back of his hand.

Doug landed against the table with a vicious thud. I glanced around the room to see if there was anything to use as a weapon. The chairs were too far away, which meant there was only…

"Hey, sir!" I yelled, grabbing a book off the case and hurling it at Mr Lee.

The teacher didn't even flinch when the book struck his face. I grabbed a big hardback and threw that. This one worked. Mr Lee loosened his grip and dropped Billy, turning to face me.

"Don't just stand there, you idiot! Run!" I screamed.

Billy took the hint and scrambled away, rubbing his bruised neck. Mr Lee started walking slowly towards me.

"This is so going to get me detention," I said, a little bit on the crazy side as I pulled the heavy old bookcase forward – straight onto Mr Lee.

The teacher looked up, as if he didn't realise the danger, and then vanished under the huge antique. The weight of the bookcase would have killed anyone human. As it was, the teacher's legs were still twitching. The bookcase was heavy though. Way too heavy to lift off, even with the books scattered across the room.

Think it was about then I went a little crazy. Not la-la crazy, but cold crazy. The crazy some of us needed just to get through those first few insane hours. It was the only way I could deal with what I'd just done.

"Dude," Kegs called out. "You killed Mr Lee. That's hardcore."

I pointed to the still-moving legs.

"I don't think so," I said.

"Now that is seriously not good," Kegs said, turning a strange colour himself. For a second I thought he was going to pass out.

"Whatever they've become, we can't kill them," I said. "You okay?"

"Yeah, course!" he bluffed. "Door!"

"Doug," I shouted. "The piano. It's the only thing strong enough to keep the door closed."

The dead on the other side were banging against it, and the door was starting to slowly inch open.

Doug, who was still slumped on the floor and dazed from the teacher's attack, pushed himself to his feet.

"Help him!" I yelled at a few terrified kids, rushing to Kegs' side and throwing my weight against the door.

A few kids were too scared to move. Too scared to do anything. They were frozen to the spot, shaking and sobbing.

"Right, that should hold them," I said, a little amazed at how normal my voice sounded. It was a heavy piano and took six of the kids to move, but once in front of the door it seemed to do the job.

"He needs a hospital," a half-Chinese kid called Charlie said. "It's a bad break."

"You don't say," Matt replied, trying to make light of the situation even though he was clearly in an amazing amount of pain. "Try and get me something to splint it, at least until we get out of here."

"Mr Lee did this?" Charlie asked.

Matt nodded. "What's going on?"

"Simple, innit? The teachers have turned into zombies and we've got to kill them all," Kegs explained.

"I don't know about that," I said. "But something bad's happened."

"Something bad?" Kegs laughed out loud. "Look at Lee. You squashed him with a bookcase and his legs are still moving. Now that's not normal behaviour – even for a teacher!"

"Bobby?" one of the Year Eights said, dropping to his knees by the side of one of the kids Mr Lee had killed.

"I'm sorry," I said, placing a hand on the kid's shoulder.

There was absolutely nothing I could say to make him feel better.

"We should chuck them out of the window," Kegs advised. "Before they come back from the dead like Jack did."

Everyone looked at the two bodies, half expecting them to move. Nothing happened.

Doug picked up a mobile and tried to dial for an ambulance. Cursing, he hurled the phone against the wall. "Why can't we get a signal?"

The piano pushed back a little and rotting arms started to force their way through the gap.

"Okay," Matt said from the side of the door. "We can't stay here. We need to get out and get some help."

"Why's Pete not back yet?" Little Jimmy stuttered.

I glanced at Kegs.

"His brother went for help," Kegs explained. "While you were upstairs. He's the fastest runner so he said he'd go to the Gatehouse. Use the phone there."

"We've got to help him," Jimmy sobbed. "He might be... he might be in trouble."

Kegs picked up a dining chair and smashed it against the wall, handing out legs to a couple of nearby kids.

"Weapons," Kegs said, looking grim. "We need weapons and this is all we've got."

Kegs walked to the gap in the door and started to bring the makeshift club down on the creatures trying to push their way through. Rotting arms retreated. Kegs dragged the piano against the door once again.

"See?" he said. "You lot, start smashing."

A few of the older kids followed Kegs' command. Within a few minutes, most of us were armed with chair legs.

"Right," Kegs said. "Let's get them."

"Wait," I warned. "We need to think this through."

"Nothing to think of. They have it coming."

"There's at least twenty monks in this place. Maybe more. Now I'm guessing they're all..."

"Zombies," Kegs interrupted.

"Changed," I continued. "Plus a couple of cooks and teachers. That means they outnumber us. And they're stronger, too."

"Pete," Jimmy repeated. "He'll have got help. He's probably waiting for us at the Gatehouse."

I glanced at Matt. We were both starting to think something bad had probably happened to Pete.

"Doubt it," Kegs stated. "He's probably dead."

Jimmy's lower lip started to tremble.

"What?" Kegs said. "You were both thinking it."

"Okay. The Gatehouse might not be such a bad idea," I said.

"What about Kelsey?" Kegs said, reminding us all about Jack. "He might still be out there."

Doug walked to the window and started smashing the glass shards from the frame while scanning the grass verge outside. It was dark.

"No sign of him," he said. "I'll go first. Alex, you go with me. Kegs, you take the rear."

"Yeah, right, so I can stay here and get all zombiefied," Kegs said. "I don't think so. I'll go first, you and your boyfriend can go last."

"Whatever. I'll help Matt. Charlie, can you give me a hand?" I said, asking one of the few Year Tens I knew.

Charlie was next to Matt, fixing two bits of broken chair to either side of his leg, some torn cloth holding them in place.

"Ironic, ain't it?" Matt grimaced. "The only one of us who knows first aid gets the broken leg."

"Okay," I said. "Kegs, you go first. The rest of you line up. Two by two and keep your eyes open. Watch for trouble. We don't know what's out there."

No one moved.

"He said get a move on!" Kegs roared, spittle flying from his mouth.

Everyone leapt to their feet.

Kegs grabbed a tablecloth, quickly folded it up and threw it over the bottom of the frame.

"For the glass," he explained.

The piano started to slide away from the door and through the gap I could see Mrs Jones trying to get in.

"Always knew she wanted me," Kegs grinned, looking back. "But all things considered, she's not my type."

I was a little surprised to see him helping kids through the window. Maybe his joking was to keep them from panic – or maybe he really was crazy. I don't know. Looking back, I do know we'd have probably died without him.

"Watch out for bits of glass," he said.

Matt let out a cry of pain as we lifted his broken leg up to get him through. There was a scraping sound back in the room and I turned to see the piano had skidded a few more yards from the door, allowing the creatures enough room to stagger through.

"They're in!" I warned, almost diving through the window. I caught one last glimpse of our school friends' bodies and then was on the move.

Kegs had run to the front, leading the group to the Gatehouse. It was only a short distance but it seemed like miles. The old oaks lining the side of the drive created even more shadows. As we moved, I scanned the darkness, half expecting to see Jack stagger out and attack us. At one point I thought saw him standing by a tree, but it all happened too quickly to be sure.

"They're trying to follow us!" I called out to the others, as we turned the corner to the Gatehouse. We were nearly there now but would soon lose sight of the main house. In the dim twilight, the creatures were framed in the light of the library, trying to walk through the window. As we watched, one of them toppled out, head first, and started to push himself to his feet. If we hadn't been so scared, it might've been comical.

We turned the corner and noticed those in front weren't going into the Gatehouse – or even trying to get in. They were just standing by the side of the main road staring straight ahead. It was only when we reached them we saw what they were looking at.

In the town, several buildings were on fire – including the block of flats just near the centre. Car alarms and burglar alarms could be heard, and mixed in to it all were the screams of kids.

"It's happening there, too," Charlie said, hope disappearing from his voice.

Kegs banged on the door.

"Door's open," he said. He was about to go in when he paused for a moment, tightening his grip on the chair leg. "Give me a sec to do a recon," he ordered, vanishing inside.

There was more noise behind us – the sound of several people shuffling down the drive towards us. Or maybe not people.

The door opened wider.

"Pete's here," Kegs said as I closed the door behind me, helping to place Matt against a wall.

"Where?" Jimmy stuttered, tears of relief appearing on his slightly chubby face.

"Through the doors, in the kitchen but…" Kegs started to say.

Jimmy wasn't listening. He rushed towards the sliding doors that divided the cottage in half. The front door led straight into the small living room; next to that was the dining room and kitchen. Jimmy opened the doors and let out a cry.

His brother was there, slumped on a chair by the kitchen table. He seemed to be in shock. He was beaten and bruised, a couple of cuts on his right arm. He was holding a dented frying pan in his hand.

"They tried to kill me," he muttered, more to himself than his brother. "I tried to stop them. I tried to kill them. But I couldn't."

"That's good," his brother said, trying to soothe Pete. "We shouldn't kill. You did the right thing."

"No, you don't understand. I tried. They just wouldn't die. No matter what I did. No matter what I hit them with – they kept attacking me."

"They were dead before they attacked you," I said. "And what happened to them?"

Pete wasn't listening, just mumbling the same words over and over again.

"Found them," Kegs shouted from the entrance to the cellar. "Looks like he threw them down here. They look a bit of a mess – I'm pretty sure they're dead. They're definitely not moving anyway, which is probably a good thing the state they're in. Nice one, Pete."

"What about the rest of the place?" I asked.

"I'll do a sweep," Kegs said, shutting the cellar door and yelling at a couple of other kids to help him.

I glanced around. The back door, leading straight from the kitchen, seemed sturdy and was bolted from the inside. I went to check the front door and heard something move outside. The door opened a little, the lock broken from where Pete must have forced his way in. I quickly pushed it shut and bolted the top and bottom. Luckily the couple were pretty security conscious. The door had a small window covered with a net curtain. I moved the curtain to one side and found myself staring out at Jack, who was dragging himself away from the Gatehouse door and looking around, confused.

It looked like his left leg and arm had been broken when he'd fallen through the window. His head, hanging eerily to one side, was moving slowly around, as though he'd lost something and was trying to find it.

"He's after us," I whispered, and saw Mr Green stagger towards him. "And he's going to lead the rest of them straight to us."

Right on cue, Jack dragged his body around so he was facing the Gatehouse. For one terrifying moment his dead, hate-filled eyes looked straight into mine.

And then he started dragging himself towards the front door. The dead followed.

THREE

"We're dead!" a kid from Year Four said from behind me.

I was about to shout at him for scaring the others when I realised he had a point.

"I don't want to die," a young kid blubbered.

"We're not going to die," I said, noticing Doug and Kegs were already searching the house.

I risked another look out of the window. More monks were staggering down the drive. Don't know why, but the sight of the dead monks was somehow scarier than our own dead teachers.

"Result," Kegs grinned, running down the stairs carrying a caddy full of golf clubs. "The caretaker played golf."

"Not the best time for a game of golf," I said, amazed at Kegs' stupidity.

"Don't be so thick," Kegs said, using his usual charm. "They're weapons now, aren't they? Good ones too. Bagsy the wood."

"What?" Billy asked.

"It's the biggest one, innit?" Kegs said. "Don't you know anything? Be better for killing the zombies. Take my advice, avoid the putter."

Billy nodded. He seemed to be making mental notes.

"We can't kill them," I said. "What if it's just some kind of

31

disease? What if there's a way of saving them?"

"Fair point but tonight's all about survival. If they attack we need to stop them and I'm guessing getting hit by a golf club will do just that," Kegs explained. "Now give me a hand with that table. I've also found the old guy's toolbox."

More dead fists started to pound on the front door.

"I hate that noise," one of the Year Eights cried. "Please make it stop."

"It's alright, it'll be fine," Billy lied.

"We need to get the legs off," I said, grabbing a saw from the caretaker's tool box.

The legs came off with relative ease (guess it must've been a cheap table). We'd just lifted it over the window and were hammering in the first few nails when a scream caught us all by surprise. It was the scream of a young girl... and it came from the cellar.

"I'll check it," I said, leaving Kegs and some of the kids to the survival D.I.Y.

"What's up?" I asked Doug and Charlie.

"Someone screamed in the cellar," Charlie said. "That's never a good thing."

"I think it was one of the bodies," Doug explained. "Maybe one of them was still alive. Well, not alive but you know what I mean..."

"Don't think they scream," I said. "And anyway, it didn't sound like a grown-up. It sounded like a kid. A really young kid."

I looked down into the cellar, flicking on the light. The two bodies were still at the foot of the stairs.

"Is someone down there?" I shouted.

No reply.

"We should check it out," I said.

"Yeah, right," Charlie laughed. "I've seen the movies. There's no way I'm going down there. First one down always gets killed."

Charlie was one of the biggest geeks at the school and a real movie buff. His dad owned the local comic shop.

"This isn't a horror film," I said.

"No, but our teachers are outside trying to kill us and one of our mates seems to have come back from the dead as some kind of zombie, so I kind of think the same rules apply."

"Quiet," I shushed, trying to listen.

There was something down there. I could hear it. The question was whether it was alive or dead.

A thought struck me.

"Wait here," I told them, rushing back into the living room.

"Problem?" Kegs asked, stopping his hammering for a moment.

I glanced at the fireplace. Or rather the mantelpiece above it. At the framed photographs. There were lots of the caretaker and his wife but on some photos they weren't alone. They were with two kids. A boy of ten or so with a mess of blond hair and a cute little girl of no more than six with a very angelic smile. She reminded me of my sister, Gabs.

"We're not as alone as we thought," I said, nodding to the photos. "I'll handle it though."

"Hello?" I shouted from the top of the cellar stairs again. "I'm Alex. I hope we didn't scare you."

No reply.

"Listen, I'm coming down, okay?"

I grabbed a golf club and took a step down, eyes focused on the bodies at the foot of the staircase. Expecting them to move at any moment. Five steps away. Four steps.

Two steps. I backed against the wall, circling the mangled bodies. Some old blankets were piled up near a disused washing machine. I used one to cover the bodies.

The cellar was a mess. Filled with old furniture and boxes. It looked like it had been someone's den once – an old and much used armchair was sitting in the centre, a small portable radio next to it. Over in the far corner, in the shadows, was an old mattress with a few boxes and bags thrown on it, a couple of dust sheets covering a ragged pile of old clothes. Elsewhere were odd parts of tools. More suitcases, box after box of papers and magazines. I nearly tripped over the wire coming from an old lawnmower and, as my hand touched the wall to steady myself, I flinched at the touch of mould underneath my fingers. The whole room smelt old and musty. It was a good place to hide. There was so much junk down there it was hard to see more than a few yards ahead.

"Hello?" I shouted out again.

Something moved on the mattresses.

"It's okay," I said, walking slowly towards them. I could just make out two shapes hiding under the dust sheets now.

"You know, when I was eight I had a friend called Michael," I whispered, trying to sound calm and friendly. "He was older than me and lived in a really old house. Every now and then we used to play in his house. He had this really old, smelly cellar. It was kind of fun but sometimes if we had a fight or something, he'd lock me in and start laughing. I used to get really scared."

A little girl pulled the dust sheet back and looked up at me suspiciously. Her brother slapped her hand and went to pull the dust sheet back over them.

"I'm sorry about your parents," I said. "We didn't know anyone else lived here. You see, we're hiding too."

The girl rolled off the mattress and onto her feet. In a split second, the boy was by her side, a rolling pin in hand for protection.

"They're not our real parents," the young girl started to explain.

"Shush," her brother warned. "Dad said you shouldn't talk to strangers."

"And he was right. You shouldn't." It was only then I realised I was still gripping the golf club. I placed it on the ground in front of me. "At least not normally," I said. "But tonight's different. This is an emergency. Bad things are happening. But you know that already, don't you?"

They both nodded.

"I'm Alex," I repeated, trying my best and most reassuring smile.

"I'm Rosie and this is my brother Christopher, but most people call him Chris," the little girl stated. "Our real parents died a long time ago. We're just staying here until we're adopted."

Chris was still eyeing me with suspicion.

"So this is your foster parents' house?" I asked.

"Yeah," Rosie said. "We call them Uncle Graham and Auntie Sheila. But they turned bad and tried to kill us and then you threw them down the stairs and broke them."

"I'm sorry about that. My best friend changed too. He became a bad person. Though I'm not sure if they're really people any more. They just look a little like them. Is your brother okay?"

Chris nodded, but he didn't look alright.

"He's upset 'cause everyone tried to kill us," Rosie explained.

"Well, that's understandable," I said. "I'm upset by that myself."

"They're not really dead, you know," Rosie added.

"I know. But they can't hurt you now," I said.

"Yes, they can," insisted Rosie, pointing behind me.

Even though I've been through a lot over the last few months, that was one of the scariest moments. It was also a moment when I thought without doubt I would soon be dead.

Charlie was right, I shouldn't have gone down to the cellar.

I picked up the golf club almost at the same moment I heard the shuffling behind me. I didn't want to look but knew I had to.

"Don't think they love us any more," Rosie sniffed, starting to cry.

Chris pulled her closer protectively.

The two corpses at the bottom of the staircase were shuffling forward, around the stairs towards us, arms outstretched. The man had somehow managed to stand, despite a badly broken arm. His dead wife was on the floor, using her arms to pull herself along.

"Christopher, can you be a good boy and take your sister upstairs please?"

"But who'll watch them?" Rosie said. "They're ill. When I was ill they stayed with me the whole time until I was all better."

"This is different," I said, trying to keep my voice calm even though my heart was beating so fast it seemed to fill the room. "They're bad people now."

They weren't listening but staring at their foster father's corpse as it came closer.

"I know. They tried to hurt us. That wasn't nice of them," Rosie said, her lower lip trembling.

"No, it wasn't, but listen, we don't have much time. That thing is not your foster father. It might look like him, but it's not. Now, why don't you go upstairs and have some ice cream or something?"

"We don't have any ice cream, silly. Uncle Graham's dyslexic."

"It's diabetic, stupid," Chris interrupted. "It means you can't eat sugar."

"I know. That must be really annoying. But please, go upstairs."

They both shook their heads and refused to move. I could almost feel the creature's breath on my back now.

Okay, so much for the subtle approach.

"Get up those stairs now!" I yelled.

Chris moved forward quickly, smacking me on the knee with the rolling pin.

"Don't shout at my sister," he said.

I cursed out loud.

"You shouldn't say that word. It's rude," Rosie told me.

I moved out to block the two zombies from reaching their kids. One corpse I might just have been able to deal with – but two? I was as good as dead.

Until Kegs appeared like a madman, baseball bat in hand, diving from the top of the staircase straight onto the zombies.

"Geronimo!" he screamed, smashing Uncle Graham off his feet.

Within seconds, Uncle Graham wasn't going to bother anyone again for a long time. Before I could react, Kegs had spun round and stopped the dead woman from getting any closer as well.

In case you're wondering, I'm not going to bother with full-on descriptions (something I guess you've already noticed). I've seen enough gratuitous violence to last a lifetime and really don't want to dwell on the blood and brains of it all. Sorry.

"Sorted," Kegs stated, dragging the zombies carefully away from the staircase, before dramatically beckoning Rosie and Chris towards the stairs with a flourish of his arms.

"Kegs…" I said, embarrassed by his inability to empathise with what the kids had been through.

I was feeling a bit shell-shocked by the whole thing and it didn't take a psychologist to work out it must've been worse for the little kids. I was also starting to get the distinct feeling Kegs might be a little bit insane.

"What?" Kegs asked, spinning the bat in his hand like it was his new favourite toy.

"The kids," I whispered, stepping closer to him and trying to keep my voice down. "So far tonight the people they love have tried to kill them and they've just seen you beat seven shades out of their dead foster parents with a rounders bat."

"What? So I should've let them kill you?" he snapped. "I can see how that would've been less traumatic for everyone. And it's not a rounders bat. It's a baseball bat. Found it upstairs behind the couch. Better than the golf club. Gave that to Billy."

"It is a rounders bat," Rosie said, moving closer and tugging at Kegs' T-shirt. "It's mine. Or will be when I get bigger. Auntie Sheila said I could…"

Rosie's lip started to tremble and she almost exploded with tears.

For the first time, Kegs looked a little guilty.

"Don't worry," he said to me. "I'll deal with this. Kids love me."

Before I could say anything, he squatted beside the crying Rosie and grim-faced Christopher.

"Hi, my name's Kegs," he said, trying his best to smile.

Maybe there was hope for him after all.

"Sorry about your foster parents. The thing is, they'd become bloodthirsty zombies and if I hadn't killed them they'd have torn you both apart."

"See, I told you," Christopher said to his sister. "I watched one of those films about zombies and could tell, but Rosie thought they were just ill."

"Listen, why don't we get upstairs?" I said, only to have the two kids ignore me and look up at Kegs.

"Come on," he said, scooping Rosie into his arms and moving towards the stairs. "There are better weapons up there anyway."

"Can I have my bat back, please?" Rosie asked.

"No," he grinned. "Finders keepers."

Chris hit him on the leg with the rolling pin.

"Okay," Kegs smiled. "But can I lend it when zombies attack?"

"Maybe," Rosie said.

"You can lend my golf clubs," Kegs said.

"Okay," she grinned.

Upstairs, Matt was in a bad way. He was paler than he'd been a few minutes before and was slumped against the wall. I tried not to think about the pain he was in or the lack of things we could do for him. I noticed a few of the kids were still trying their mobiles. Most had decided to give Matt space and were spread out through the living room and kitchen. Doug was getting a few of the older ones to help fortify the house. It seemed to be working. For a while it was nice to hear the hammering. It drowned out the sound of dead fists pounding on the front door.

"I don't know what to do about Matt," Charlie said. "I think he needs a hospital."

"Yeah, but we can't get out of the house," I reminded him. "What do you think's happened?"

"I never thought I'd say this," Charlie said. "But I think Kegs is right. I think they really are zombies."

"If they are… dead, why hasn't everyone changed? And how come we can kill them?"

"Anything dies if you hit it enough," Kegs said, adding a wink to Chris, "You should remember that next time."

Chris nodded as though he was making mental notes of everything Kegs said.

"Why don't you see if it's on the TV?" Rosie said. "It's not a good TV and only has a few channels, but it might be on the news. Uncle Graham's always watching the news. Says he likes to keep informed."

A few of us looked at each other as though wondering why we hadn't thought of that. Charlie, who was nearest, flicked it on.

I was a little surprised when Coronation Street appeared. It was surreal, something like the end of the world happening outside and a soap opera on TV. Charlie flicked through the channels. It was the same all over. The regular programmes on. No news.

"It's *The Simpsons*," Rosie said. "I like them."

"Me too," Kegs said, squatting by his two new friends.

I glanced at Doug.

"Looks normal enough," I said.

"Yeah," Doug agreed. "Maybe it was just round here."

"Like a curse or something?" I suggested. "Sounds a bit far-fetched."

"So does all our teachers and a bunch of monks turning into killer zombies."

"Good point," I said, just as Matt let out a cry of pain.

"I'm alright," he smiled. "Well, you know. Apart from the constant agony."

"We'll get you help," I said. "Hang in there."

"I've got a plan," Doug whispered to me. "The back of the house is clear of zombies. For some reason they're all out front. I think they're too stupid to think of trying the back door. I can get out that way and get some help."

"What if there's no help to get?" I suggested. "Looked like things were bad in town as well."

"Think we should try. Worst case scenario, we'll know just how bad it is," Doug said.

"True," I replied. "But I don't think you should go alone. If a few of us go, we'll be able to watch out for each other."

I tried to ignore the voice inside my head. The voice calling me an idiot for even thinking of leaving the safety of the house.

"Makes sense," Doug said.

I explained our plan to the others. Kegs was going to join us but Rosie started crying.

"Think I better stay," he said. "I'll keep a look out for you. Don't be too long."

"I'll come as well," Charlie said.

Doug looked at him and smiled.

"Hey, we're mates. Mates stick together," Charlie smiled back.

Kegs opened the back door. It was dark now.

Suddenly, it didn't seem the greatest plan in the world.

"Be safe," Kegs said, closing the door behind us.

And then the three of us were standing there – with the dead less than twenty yards away from us.

FOUR

"I've got a red shirt on," Charlie whispered, as the door closed behind us. "That's not good. The guy with the red shirt always gets killed."

"He does if he keeps talking," I said. "And anyway, I've got a red shirt on too and I have no intention of dying."

Charlie mumbled something and moved behind me to walk next to Doug. He was freaked out and there was no way I could blame him for that. I was myself.

We'd planned our route before leaving and worked out that we could go down a grass verge that lay behind the Gatehouse. With a bit of luck, the Gatehouse itself would block the zombies' view of us until we were safely over the wall and on the main road beyond.

"So far, so good," Doug whispered as we managed to reach the wall without incident.

Once over, we set off down the deserted road, the old Victorian houses to either side rising above us like gravestones. It was dark now, although a full moon was shining brightly down on everything and the street lights were still working – but the scent of smoke was heavy in the air and flames could be seen in the distance in the town centre.

"Not sure this was such a great idea after all," I said, as we turned a corner. The road wound down into the town's main street. As we walked, I got the distinct feeling we were being watched.

"The cops," Charlie said, catching sight of a police car parked by the side of the road a little way ahead of us, its lights still flashing. "We can get help."

"Wait," I warned, taking in the scene.

It was hard to see what was happening from this distance, but it looked like a policeman was standing with his back to us by the side of his car, talking to some homeless guy.

"It'll be fine," Charlie said, running towards him. "Hey, officer! Over here. We need your help!"

"This ain't right," Doug said beside me. "They always travel in pairs."

I glanced at Doug suspiciously.

"Oh come on, you must've heard about it? I got caught joyriding last year just after my folks split up. The point is, I know they always send them out in pairs. It's for safety. So where's his mate?"

My hand tightened around the golf club. We both stepped forward slowly and I raised the torch, flicking it on to illuminate the cop.

"Officer," we heard Charlie say as we got closer. "Did you hear me? We need your… help."

Charlie's request caught in his throat as the cop turned round, his dead bluish-grey skin illuminated in the torchlight. Worse still, what I thought had been a homeless guy was another kid. A young kid of no more than twelve, struggling in the cop's rotting right hand.

"Charlie, run!" I yelled.

But Charlie was too close to run. The cop backhanded him and Charlie was thrown with a brutal slam against the side of a car.

"You okay?" I asked, reaching him a moment later.

"Knew I was going to die," he mumbled.

There was a sound of snapping bone and we both looked to see the cop drop the now dead boy to the floor and turn to face us.

"We've got to get out of here," I said.

"No," Doug said, stopping me. "What we need is to get in the car."

"What?"

"The car, I can drive it."

The cop was only a few yards away now. There was no time to argue – especially as Doug had already climbed into the driver's seat and was starting the ignition. We jumped in, slamming the doors behind us. I was in the passenger seat, Charlie in the back. Within seconds, the dead cop was smashing his dead hands on the roof. With death so close, there was only one thing the car could do.

It stalled.

"I thought you said you could drive?" I shouted.

"First time in a cop car," Doug said. "Well, first time in the front of a cop car!"

"Now would be a really good time to go," I urged.

"Got it," Doug grinned as the car growled into life. He reversed quickly before taking off down the road, the cop falling to the ground as we moved off.

"Let's just get back to the Gatehouse," I said.

"Might be a problem with that," Charlie said.

I glanced back and my heart sank. An old woman was staggering down the road towards us, her dressing gown blowing in the wind, one of her slippers missing, her skin that now familiar blue-grey of the creatures trying to kill us. Others were joining her and stumbling after us.

"Old people freak me out," Doug said. "Especially when they're trying to kill me."

With the road behind us blocked by the dead, we had no real alternative but to press on to the centre of town – in the vague hope that there might be some signs of life there.

As soon as we got close, we knew our hopes were in vain. The dead were everywhere, some slumped against the walls of shops, others walking along as though they couldn't quite remember who or what they were. Sometimes the dead seemed to be fighting over corpses. A few kids could be seen lying dead on the ground. The odd shop window had been smashed, and at least two restaurants were on fire, the flames spreading to other buildings nearby. One of the dead walked from a burning building, oblivious to the flames consuming his body. One thing united the dead. As our car passed, they turned and started to follow us.

Doug turned out to be a good driver, which was just as well as he had both the walking dead and abandoned cars to avoid.

"If the map was right, the hospital should just be over the bridge," Doug said. "Maybe they were okay there…"

All three of us knew that wouldn't be the case. But with the dead following, we had to press on. At least until we could think of something better to do. A building was burning ahead of us. We knew what it was before we even reached the bridge.

"Looks like the hospital's closed," Doug said, pulling up on the road outside the building. A few of the dead, damaged by the flames, started to bang on the car.

"Better get moving," I suggested. "If the flames get to the car…"

"Yeah," Charlie agreed. "And there's nothing for us here. Nothing at all."

"Problem with heading back though," Doug said, turning the corner quickly to shake off a dead doctor trying to get into the car. "The only way back is the way we've come – and that's now filled with…"

Doug paused for a moment like he didn't know what word to use.

"I really don't want to use the Z-word but that's what they are, isn't it?"

"Yeah," Charlie said. "Looks that way."

"Try and get us up there," I said, pointing to a road leading onto the moors.

The town was big enough to help us get some distance between ourselves and the stiffs by the time we hit the road leading to the moors. Once there, Doug cut the lights and started to move slower.

"Think this might be the best place to stop," he said, pulling the car over to the side of the road.

We could see the lights of the monastery ahead of us. The road curled away from the back of it. Doug was right, this was the closest point. Just a quick walk in the darkness across the edge of the moors towards the Gatehouse – right past a zombie-filled monastery.

"What do you reckon?" I asked. "Five minutes' walk?"

"Maybe ten," Doug said. "We need to be careful."

I was about to say something else when Charlie motioned me to be quiet, pointing to two creatures slowly moving up the road we'd just taken. We nodded and set off across the long bushy grass. Even if we didn't have to be quiet we would've been. All our thoughts were the same. If this was happening all over the town, the chances were it was happening everywhere else as well – including back home. We stopped for a while at the edge of the moors. The lights were still on in the Retreat and we could see the dead shuffling around inside the old building – and those still trying to get into the Gatehouse. The oaks lining the driveway made it hard to see clearly, but the number of dead seemed to have doubled since we'd left. Not a good sign.

"Think we should circle around," I suggested. "Stay low so they can't see us. That way we should end up near the back again."

The others nodded. I was thankful for the moonlight. At least it gave us a chance to see where we were walking. We'd been wrong about the time. It wasn't five or ten minutes. Creeping across the moorland took us the better part of an hour. We were scared. Scared that the dead would see us and that would be it. The dead behind us were still on our track as well. They'd reached the abandoned car and were now moving onto the moor.

The wall around the Retreat was about waist height and led to a car park. The odd creature could be seen now, shambling around the Retreat's grounds. The Gatehouse was less than thirty yards away. I pulled out the torch and flashed it on and off. No response from the house.

We moved off towards the back door, walking slowly but purposefully across the car park. Hoping our friends would see the torch and open the back door before the dead heard us approach. We were halfway there when the James Bond theme started blasting from my jeans pocket. For a second I didn't know what it was. The three of us actually laughed. A sort of what-is-that kind of laugh. Then I remembered it was my phone, and we all remembered the zombies were dumb but could be attracted by sight and noise and suddenly it wasn't very funny. I grabbed my phone. The name on the display was Gabs – my kid sister!

"Quiet," Charlie whispered. "You're going to get us all killed."

But it was too late to be quiet. The dead were already starting to melt away from the front of the house to investigate the new noise at the rear.

"Alex, I'm scared," my sister's voice sobbed on the phone.

She sounded so fragile and broken. My fear for her went to all-new heights. "Mummy tried to hurt me. I was about to go to Johnny's but the car wouldn't start and then Mummy stopped moving and then she tried to… She tried to…"

Gabs burst into tears.

"I'm scared, Alex. I'm really scared."

Her words left me cold. Mummy tried to hurt me. My mum. She was one of them. A zombie.

"I'm coming home," I said. "I'm coming home and it'll all be fine. But until I get home you've got to find somewhere to hide – and don't talk to anyone, okay? Even if you think it's someone you know like Dad or Uncle Dan. Okay?"

"Okay," she whispered. "Please hurry though. I'm scared. I…"

The line went dead.

"No!" I shouted, trying to call back.

"Alex, come on!" Charlie and Doug urged from a few yards away.

Charlie grabbed my arm. I looked back over the moors to the cop car. More zombies were there but I didn't care, I had to get home. I had to help my sister.

"We've got to go," I said to Doug. "You need to drive me home. My sister…"

"Alex, come on," he urged. "It's pointless."

"Let me go!" I shouted, trying to shake off his grip.

"You're not thinking straight," Doug said, glancing around at the dead who were getting closer with every passing second.

"It's my sister!" I yelled.

Doug looked around.

"Great," he said. "Nice one. They've beat us to the back door now. No way we can get in and no way we can get back to the car. You've only gone and killed us. Cheers."

I didn't know what to say. My sister's voice was still the only thing in my mind. Even with the dead all around us.

"Red shirts," Charlie mumbled, looking at our clothes. He saw Doug's black hoodie and added, "Bet you outlive us both."

"We'll have to smash our way through," I said. "We can do it. We have golf clubs."

They looked at me as if I was stupid.

"Unless either of you have a better plan?"

"Some school trip," Doug smiled. "Let's do it."

Within ten yards the first zombie was on us. Doug was the fastest and seemed to find the violence the easiest to deal with. Charlie was terrified but trying his best. I still wasn't really there but knew one thing. I had to survive. I had to survive so I could save Gabs.

The back door was so far away though – and more creatures

were moving into view. The three of us paused for a moment, all realising the same horrific fact at the same time.

"We're not going to make it," Doug said. "There's too many."

"And my asthma's playing up," Charlie wheezed. "Remind me not to leave my inhaler in the Retreat again, will you?"

There must have been thirty around us. Maybe more. It was hard to tell in the shadows.

"Sorry about the phone," I said. "And the getting us all killed."

"Forget it," Doug said, then cursed, "Sod it. I'm not just going to stand here and let them surround us. Let's give it one last try. Even if it is hopeless."

"Sounds like a plan," I smiled.

"Not much of one," Charlie added, smiling sadly.

We rushed forward together. Within yards the creatures were on us. Charlie was the first to fall, stumbling over. Two corpses were on him straight away, grabbing and punching him. I could almost feel their hatred of the living.

"Charlie!" Doug shouted, heading towards his friend.

I tried to shout a warning but, before I could, found myself under attack from a dead monk. A backhand knocked me from my feet, the tarmac scraping my hands as I hit the floor hard. I was on my knees, about to push myself up when a dead fist punched the back of my head, sending me down again. The world started to spin away from me. Before I passed out I remember thinking how weird it was that the last sound I would ever hear was a kid shouting one word.

"Geronimo!"

FIVE

There was a moment when I had the strangest feeling of waking from a dream and felt certain that I was at home and my mum was calling me for school.

"Welcome back to the land of the living," Matt said from opposite me.

We were both on mattresses on the floor of the dining room. A few candles were burning on a small coffee table. Someone had made a much better splint for Matt's leg, a couple of broom handles tied with strong black electrician's tape. But he wasn't in a good way. I got the feeling it was taking all his will power to hide just how much pain he was in.

Most people were in the living room. A few were hugging their knees and staring into space. There was a noise that sounded like a broken tractor trying to start. It took me a few moments to realise it was Kegs, snoring his head off, Christopher and Rosie asleep by his side. Pete was in the corner, trying to get an old computer to work.

"Who's keeping watch?" I asked.

"A kid called Paul and his mate are upstairs checking the front. Jimmy at the back." Matt flinched, clutching his leg.

"How is it?" I asked.

"Hurts. They found some painkillers and made a splint but…"

"We're all going to get through this," I said.

"Listen," Matt grimaced. "With me like this and Jack, well, with Jack gone, you're the oldest. They'll be looking to you."

"I'm not the oldest," I said, terrified by the thought of people relying on me. "There's…"

"Kegs?" Matt laughed. "We're doomed. Anyway, you are older than him. He's just bigger and more prone to violence than you."

"It'll be over soon," I said. "Whatever it is that's happening. I bet even now people are trying to get help to us."

"We'll see," Matt said, as Jimmy rushed in.

"The internet, we've got the internet," Jimmy interrupted, eyes wide with excitement.

Still feeling a little dizzy, I found myself using the wall for support as I stood up.

I glanced across the room to see other kids were gathering around Pete and the computer.

"We're online," Pete said. "Phones worked for a few seconds but went dead again. The house has cable though and this really old PC. Took me a while to crack the password but we're in now."

"It was 'Rosie'," Rosie said with a sad smile.

"Now, let's see what's going on," Pete said, going to the BBC News page.

"Not been updated," he said. While searching he also downloaded his email.

"There's some from back home," he said, "Sent in the last

53

hour, too."

"Maybe it's not everywhere," a young kid said from behind me.

Pete went pale.

"It's my cousin," he said, his voice almost trembling. "Or one of them anyway. Listen… 'Pete are you there? Dad's changed into something and tried to kill me. It's like he's gone insane. I'm hiding in my bedroom but I can hear him on the other side of the door, banging against it. I don't know what to do. He's different. I tried to call the police but all the phones are engaged or not working. I can hear the door… it sounds like it's about to break open. I'm scared."

Pete looked up at us all, his eyes clouding over.

"That's all it says," he said. "There's a few more. Here's one from Johnny. Some kind of group email by the look of it: 'Something bad's happened. Happening. Everyone over eighteen's changed into… well we think they've died and become some kind of zombie. We know that sounds crazy but you probably know it's true. Dad tried to kill me. Bill's injured. Badly injured and we can't get an ambulance for him. We've done our best but I think he's going to die. We're clearing out the main hall. If you can make your way here, do. Bring food if you can. We have weapons and the building's secure. At least for now. Will try and update later – if everything's still working. Matt, if you read this, I hope you're safe. And I hope you can forgive me for Dad. I didn't have a choice. I'm going out soon to try and get sis back here. If I don't see you again, I'm sorry. Maybe Dad was right, maybe I just wasn't good enough…"

"Jack was eighteen today," I said. Not that anyone needed

reminding of the fact.

"There's clips on YouTube," Pete said. "And some footage on Facebook."

Pete clicked on a video link.

The first was from London, somewhere near the centre. The kid must've come from a rich family because you could see the north bank of the Thames and the Houses of Parliament. The hotel above Charing Cross station was burning – a full-on inferno – as were other buildings along the Thames. Somehow worse than the grainy image of the destruction was the voiceover that went with it. It was a girl, just a teenager. She wasn't crying and hysterical but had a cold and distant calm in the way she spoke that suggested part of her mind had gone.

"I'm dead," she stated. "They're here, all of them. Mum, Dad, Charlotte. They're going to get me. Unless I climb out of the balcony and… well, we're six storeys up. I just wanted to show you this before I go. I saw the others online and, I don't know, I guess I just wanted to leave something of myself behind. I was in my room when it happened. I'd just argued with my parents about being pregnant and… I've got to go. My name's Claire Janson. I'm sixteen and I don't know what's going to happen. I can't see a way out of this. Not a good one anyway."

The clip stopped.

The next was from some small American town, couldn't tell which one. A kid was filming from his bedroom window. He sounded about fifteen and his voice was mixed in with the sound of sirens and screams. He was laughing – like he was actually enjoying it all. But the more we listened, the less sane he sounded.

"I didn't go to church," he said with a broken laugh. "I think that saved my life. Looks like a bad zombie flick down there. They're killing anyone they find. Any kids, that is. Look at that one. Hey you, Four Eyes, behind you!"

The video showed some young kid, maybe thirteen, running down the street, but stopping when he heard the shout. He was trying to run in between the creatures but was clearly exhausted. One of them caught up with him, grabbing him from behind as the others moved in for the kill.

"That's got to hurt," the first kid's voice laughed. "My folks are at church. Did I tell you that? They're probably like everyone else now. Hey, the store's on fire. How cool is that!"

Pete stopped the link and whispered a few swearwords about the kid under his breath before clicking on a couple of more. Narrow Parisian avenues with the dead rushing through like a mob of rioters. I don't speak French, but when a kid who looked Algerian showed the image of his dead brother and sister, I got the gist of it. Moscow, Prague, Tokyo, Sydney. The last one was weird. It was afternoon there, the link showing footage of the beach. It looked a beautiful day, but in the midst of it zombies in trunks were dragging a young kid along the sand, leaving red behind them. Pete spent the next few minutes searching for anything that could suggest somewhere life was still going as normal, but there was nothing.

"Better save the power," he said, turning the computer off and whispering to me, "It's the same everywhere, no point scaring the kids."

I nodded.

"You okay?" Pete asked.

"Not really," I answered. "Who could be?"

"Something's happening," Paul said, running down the stairs. "I think it might be help."

A few of us rushed up to the top bedroom. Looking out of the bedroom window, we could see the main road we'd gone down earlier. The first light of dawn was already starting to break out. There was a sound as well. An engine, getting closer and closer.

"It's a car," someone shouted. "Maybe it's the army."

Below, the creatures were also starting to slowly turn their heads to the sound. Some broke rank and shambled towards it.

"Sounds more like a truck," I suggested. "Or a bus."

"Close," Charlie said, as a coach, swerving like mad on the road, lights shining out in front, crashed around the corner and zoomed towards us, ploughing through any of the creatures who dared to stand in its way.

"It's going to crash!" someone shouted.

"No, it's not," I said. "And I've seen it before."

I almost leapt down the stairs, the others following me. "Everyone grab what you can right now. We have a coach to catch."

"What about Matt?" Charlie said. "We can't just leave him."

"There's an old wheelbarrow in the cellar. Get him in it and give him a club. When we clear a path, I'll yell and you can wheel him out."

Charlie nodded and rushed downstairs. I started trying to tear the barricades off the front door.

"Kegs, give us a hand!"

Kegs was still half asleep, but together we managed to get the old table down just as some more kids rushed down the stairs.

"It's stopped near the drive," a young kid said, his voice filled with hope. "And it's full of girls!"

There was something about the way he said "girls" that made me laugh.

"You can borrow my rounders bat if you want," Rosie said to Kegs.

"Thanks," Kegs replied, handing her his golf club and adding under his breath, "but it's a baseball bat."

"No, it's not," Rosie sulked.

"Whatever," Kegs said. "Now, when we get out there what are you two going to do?"

"Stay close to you unless you get killed, in which case we're going to run and hide," they both said, Rosie adding, "But you're not going to get deaded, are you?"

"Nah, I'm too good-looking to die."

Christopher found this statement really funny. For my part I was just amazed how well they were handling things.

"Everyone here?" I checked, as Charlie appeared with the wheelbarrow.

"This has got to be the worst wheelchair ever," Matt said, trying to make light of the situation as Doug and Charlie lifted him into it.

"Okay," I explained. "Youngest in the middle. Everyone else front and back. Head straight for the coach. Ready? One, two…"

I opened the door and found myself eye to eye with Jack. I shoulder-charged him out of the way, sending him flying backwards. He landed about five or six yards from the door. I ignored him and started to run. A monk was at my side and I swung the golf club, striking his shoulder. The creature didn't

even flinch, and tried to grab my club. Luckily, Pete had my back and brought his own club straight down onto the creature's head. It fell to the ground and struggled to get back up. I could see the coach about ten yards ahead, girls shouting from the windows, urging us on. It was the girls we'd met the day before. Seemed like a lifetime ago.

"There's too many!" Pete shouted by my side. A kid cried out, and I risked a glance back to see one of the Year Nines being lifted off his feet by a creature and hurled against a nearby tree. His body slumped against it. A kid from Year Seven called Greg went to try and help him. I yelled that it was no use, but couldn't reach him in time. The kid shouted that the Year Nine boy was dead, only to be killed himself seconds later. We were so close to the coach, but the creatures had us surrounded. There had to be at least twenty of them just in between us and the doors and more to our sides and back. I heard another scream and saw Billy go down under a crowd of zombies – only to have two other kids smash their way through and rescue him. They somehow managed to get the dazed and semi-conscious Billy from the pack of zombies and drag him to the coach. Seeing a bit of clear space, Charlie came rushing out of the house with Matt, Doug behind him. On the wheelbarrow an insane-looking Matt was screaming for all he was worth and swinging the golf club around his head like crazy. For a second I thought he was going to hit Charlie, but he didn't and even managed to get a couple of the creatures. Doug had Charlie's back, his grim determination reminding me of some film I'd seen about gladiators. Not that gladiators used golf clubs or fought zombies.

"Back to back!" Kegs yelled, "Like in a war movie!"

Somehow we all knew what he meant. We made sure Matt and the kids were in the middle and started swinging our clubs and makeshift bats as best we could. For a few precious seconds we were keeping them at bay. There seemed to be some commotion on the bus too, and for a second I thought some zombies might've got on board. Instead I could see Cara and Kim screaming at another, slightly older girl. I felt something grab my shoulder and realised it was a monk's cold, dead hand.

"I don't think so," I snarled, bringing the club down on the arm. The zombie's eyes were on fire with hatred. Pete and someone else dragged me away and pushed me towards the coach, where Cara and Kim had rushed out to help us create a path through.

"Quick!" Kim yelled, looking like some kind of crazed Amazonian warrior. "Or do you want to walk?"

"Think I'm in love," Kegs said, rushing towards the door, bat in one arm, Rosie under the other, the young Christopher in front.

"Thought you might need a lift," Kim smiled, helping Kegs get Rosie and Chris onto the coach.

"Come on!" Kegs yelled, rushing back to the door to help others on board. "Last one in's a zombie."

Charlie was next to reach the door, wheelbarrow in front of him. Matt was obviously in agony as a couple of the girls and Kegs helped lift him out of the wheelbarrow and into a seat. Sweat was pouring down his face and I had the feeling the pain had just got even worse.

The coach's engines roared and it moved forward a little, giving us all a shock.

"You can't even drive, Laura, so don't be a stupid cow," Kim screamed, adding in a calmer but scarier voice, "Get away from the wheel or I'll kill you."

At the time it didn't dawn on me that it was the same girl she'd been arguing with earlier.

The last of the kids were almost on now. Cara was near me, scanning everyone with a look of increasing desperation.

"Where's Jack?" she said.

"I'm sorry," I said, stepping towards the coach.

Only Kim, Kegs, Cara and me were still outside the coach now, the dead moving towards us en masse. Tears started pouring down Cara's face. I'd never seen anyone's heart break before but I'm pretty sure that's what was happening right there and then.

"No, I don't believe it!" she cried.

"It was his birthday. He was eighteen," I tried to explain, aware of how close the dead were getting.

"I know that," she cried. "I was going to sneak out and meet him. He can't be dead. He…"

She looked up and caught sight of his broken body standing by the Gatehouse, staring at us all with nothing but hatred and death in his eyes.

"Jack, quick. We're about to leave!" Cara shouted, rushing forward to try and reach him. Kegs and me managed to block her, Kegs gaining a nasty scratch on his cheek for his trouble. Something grabbed me around my neck – with my back turned trying to stop Cara I'd left myself wide open to attack. I tried to turn and saw Mrs Jones attacking me. It was hard to believe I once had a crush on her. Kim was by my side, bringing a hockey stick down on the teacher.

"Cara, he's one of them," Kim urged, trying to drag her friend toward the coach.

Another zombie made a grab for her, only to be blocked and beaten by Kegs. Cara was hysterical. I looked across at Jack – or the thing that had once been Jack – and it might've just been my imagination, but for a second the hate seemed to leave his eyes, replaced by a haunted and pained expression of loss.

"We don't have time for this," Kim said, and punched her friend in the face.

At first I thought she'd killed Cara.

"Quick, give me a hand," she said.

Together we managed to lift her unconscious friend on to the coach. Kegs smacked one last zombie out of the way before backing up the stairs.

"All aboard!" The girl in the driver's seat grinned. It was one of those grins I was starting to recognise. One that said, "This whole thing's made me a little bit crazy and insane."

Her name was Molly Reynolds (seventeen, redhead, worked on her father's farm during the summer. Real life-saver, that – especially the driving a tractor part).

"Buckle up, this could get bumpy. Especially as I'm still learning to drive."

"You're doing fine," Kim said, standing by her side.

"Any idea where we're going?" I asked, trying to stand in between the seats only to nearly fall over when we went over something dead.

"The White Stones Hotel," Kim said. "We've got a baby to save."

SIX

"It was a gamble," Kim explained as the coach headed along the road, swerving to avoid an abandoned car. "You see, we need your help."

"How?" I asked, glancing back at my friends.

The elation I'd felt, that we'd all felt, after making it to the coach had vanished in an instant when Paul Wallace (thirteen, liked cricket and bad American comedy films) asked where his friend Kev was. It didn't take long to work out Kev hadn't made it. He was the kid who had died (along with Greg) as we'd fought our way from the house. Everyone on the coach looked shell-shocked and haunted. Now that the immediate threat had passed, people were starting to try and work out what had just happened. A few looked like they might have lost their minds for a while and were mumbling to themselves incoherently. Most just stared emotionlessly into space or out of the window. A few were sobbing quietly. Some of the kids were even helping those in a worse state, trying to tell them it would be okay. That everything would be okay.

They were lying of course. But right there and then it seemed lies were the only hope we had left.

For my part, I was worrying about my sister. I'd sent her a

text, telling her to hide or try to get to the TA Centre – perhaps the safest place in town – but the thought of her alone…

It was hard, but I knew I couldn't panic. If I started to panic, or to think just how much danger my sister was in, I'd drown in the fear and then be no use to anyone – especially Gabs.

As we drove along the road that cut through the moors above the town, I pressed my forehead against the window, looking out over the bushes and grassland as the first light of day tried to break through. It was beautiful. In that moment away from the death and destruction, sitting quietly on the coach and looking out over the moors, the clouds were a brilliant red. I was amazed how something so beautiful could exist when there was so much horror around us.

"There's a house at the end of this road, a hotel for hikers and tourists," Kim said. "It belongs to Laura's parents."

I didn't answer. The chances were that her parents were dead.

"There's a restaurant, too, part of the hotel, that Laura reckons could be pretty much full on a Bank Holiday Friday – that's about twenty people. Plus a couple of cooks and two waitresses. There are eight bedrooms, but if we're lucky they'd have been empty at the time it happened."

"Sounds like a deathtrap," I said. "Especially now. You're saying there could be more than thirty of those creatures in there."

Kim nodded. "And Laura's kid brother, Danny. He's six months old."

The horror of the night suddenly grew worse.

"Laura tried getting through earlier but couldn't. Most of our friends haven't made it. When we got back to the school…"

Kim paused for a second and looked like someone on the edge of collapsing into a broken heap. There was blood on her white school shirt. Dried blood. When we'd seen them earlier that day, the coach had been full of girls from the school. Now there were just eight of them.

"Laura's not talked much since we found her," Kim continued, after a deep breath. "Two of our friends went with her, but they didn't come back. With just the eight of us, there's not much chance of getting in there. Cara was desperate to help you, well, to help Jack anyway."

I glanced at Cara. She hadn't said a word since seeing Jack. She was blank and emotionless, nothing left inside her.

"So we thought if we could get you, maybe you could help us get the baby. Or at least try to."

I got the feeling there was far more to her story, but there and then I could only think about what she'd just said.

A baby.

Laura was near us and looked up.

"Please…" she whispered, in a broken voice.

Her mascara had run down the sides of her face, her long dark hair making her look like some strange Goth. On another day, she'd have been classically beautiful. That morning, she was trembling with fear and worry. Not for herself, though. For her baby brother.

"Think we should stop here," Molly said, bringing the coach to a halt. "Don't want to get too close in case they hear us."

"This hotel could be good," Charlie said, joining us at the front. "Okay, so it could be full of those… those creatures. But if we could get rid of them. Well, it could be a good place to hole up for a while."

"I need to get home," I said. "My sister."

"I know," Charlie said. "And you're not the only one. We've all got people back home, but if we don't take a moment to regroup… To get some rest and find some food… Well, I don't think we'll all make it."

As much as I hated to admit it, Charlie had a point.

"Who goes in?" I asked.

"It's a free world," Charlie said. "Figure whoever wants to."

"We'll need someone to stay with Matt," I stated, looking towards the back seat where our friend was lying down. Every now and again he'd yell out in pain – and apologise straight after.

Most wanted to go. Some were scared of being left on their own, some just needed to do something, and some (and as much as I hate to admit it, I was in this latter group) just wanted to hurt these things as much as they'd hurt us.

The plan was simple. A small group of us would sneak up the fire escape while the others distracted the zombies in the restaurant. Pete had scouted the scene. It was bad. Lots of dead in the restaurant looking confused, a couple in the corridor on the first floor (Pete had gone up the fire escape to check). The first part of the plan went fine. We carefully crept up the staircase, acutely aware of just how much noise we seemed to be making – especially when the world around us, devoid of cars and people, was so quiet. I found myself taking the lead,

Laura, Kim, Pete and Billy behind me. Kegs was leading the main posse to the restaurant. They'd make noise outside to distract the dead.

There was a small window underneath the fire escape looking into the restaurant. I'd risked a glance inside and noticed about ten of the creatures standing still, looking at a doorway leading upstairs. A few tables had been overturned. The restaurant looked like some kind of mini riot had taken place there. A couple of kids lay dead by one of the overturned tables. I listened closely and thought I could hear a baby crying from near the top of the house.

"It's the door to the staircase," Laura whispered from just behind me. "They're watching the door. I bet Trish locked it when she went upstairs…"

Trish was Laura's closest friend. Like a sister, apparently. Same age, almost the same appearance. She worked for Laura's mum in the school holidays.

Laura paused for a moment as we reached the top of the fire escape. Through the fire door, we could see into the corridor. Two zombies were wandering down the corridor, like drunken security guards. Slumped against the wall was a dead girl about our own age.

"Trish," Laura whispered.

I glanced back at Charlie, who was at the bottom of the staircase, to check everyone was in position. He nodded and gave me the okay sign.

It was time.

"Okay, here we go," I said, bringing the handle of the golf club straight into the glass of the fire door.

The burglar alarm started crying out.

"So much for the element of surprise," I said, quickly putting my arm through the hole made by the broken glass to try and open the fire door. A shard of glass sliced into my forearm. Hearing the glass smash, the two dead turned to face us, a now familiar breathless growl coming from their rotting throats.

The security bar wouldn't budge. I pushed hard, ignoring the blood flowing down my forearm. Once, twice, three times. Nothing. The zombies were getting closer. I gave it one last try.

"About time," Laura said, pushing past me as the door opened and running towards the zombies, her hockey stick swinging madly.

I was about to follow when Kim stopped me, wrapping a torn bit of cloth from her blouse around my bleeding forearm.

"It'll do for now," she said, rushing after Laura.

The first zombie didn't last long. It looked like it had been a bearded walker in his mid to late forties before the Change.

A second bearded walker avoided Laura's club, his flabby rotting arms snaking out quickly and grabbing her throat.

Only two of us could attack in the corridor at any one time and even then we couldn't swing our clubs properly. Ignoring the pain (and the fact that the white makeshift bandage was already red with my own blood) I brought my own club down on the zombie's arms, trying to loosen its deadly grip on Laura – but it was no use. The cut was making my strike weak, and even though I could hear bone break in the creature's arms it didn't loosen its grip. I tried again, this time bringing the club down on the creature's head, and it collapsed to the floor, twitching.

There was a constant thudding from the door downstairs now, coupled with the angry snarls of zombies and the screams of our friends as they created a distraction, trying to draw the creatures away from trying to get up the stairs to us. Not that it was working. There was a splintering crash of breaking wood and I knew for certain the door had caved in – and the zombies were starting to make their way up to us. Looking down the corridor, three more bedroom doors were wide open. The staircase at the end led to the converted attic Laura's family used as a lounge and bedrooms. It seemed further away than ever – especially when two creatures staggered out of the room nearest to it. One was a young woman who'd been dressed to kill. I guess was still dressed to kill, but death and the sudden decomposition had really damaged her looks. A dead, balding businessman staggered out of the room after her. He looked like he might have once played rugby but then let himself go. The girl turned her attention towards us, as the man turned towards the open door to the attic. Just then a new sound could be heard under the chaos – a baby crying.

"Danny!" Laura screamed, trying to get past me.

I rushed the girl zombie, knocking her over. Two more appeared on the landing – the first to make it up from the restaurant. Both had been men in their early twenties, dressed for a night on the town.

It was all going wrong. With the door open from the restaurant, other zombies were moving towards the staircase. Kegs' attempt at distracting them had failed.

Then I heard it. The familiar roar.

"Geronimo!" Kegs and the others were in the restaurant. I couldn't see what was going on, but from the screams it seemed that quite a few of the kids had decided the best way to distract the zombies was to attack them. It worked, as well. Suddenly the dead had other things to do than reach the staircase.

Billy rushed to my side, smacking his club down onto a fallen zombie, just missing my head by a whisker. Judging by the manic look in his eyes and the mad cry as he attacked, he'd lost it big time. Charlie and Doug rushed past to help the girls. The corridor widened at the top of the staircase and they stood their ground, smashing one of the dead men against the other and sending both tumbling back down the stairs towards the restaurant. All was chaos, the alarm and crying baby somehow making it all far more of a nightmare.

"Stay here," I said to Charlie and Doug. "Try to stop them following us."

They nodded, both tightening their grips on their clubs as the zombie they had pushed back was dragging itself to its feet, only to collapse, its right leg broken.

Laura and Kim rushed up the stairs before I could tell them to be careful. I followed quickly, Billy close behind me. I almost ran straight into the back of the girls as I reached the top. The staircase led straight into the corner of a converted living room, a couple of bedrooms leading off. One was Laura's, the other her parents' – where the baby was crying. The zombie that had made the stairs was almost in the master bedroom now, but another was blocking Laura and Kim. Tall and thin, with short dark hair, there was something vaguely familiar about it.

"What are you waiting for?" I shouted. "Hit it."

"Daddy?" Laura sobbed, sounding younger than Rosie. "Don't. Please..."

"It's not your father, Laura," Kim said, raising her hockey stick. "Your father's dead."

"No, you can't," Laura cried, blocking Kim, stepping in between her and her father.

I couldn't even get in the room, blocked as I was at the top of the staircase.

"Laura!" I cried out.

Too late.

Laura's dead father grabbed his daughter and hurled her against the wall. She slumped down and didn't move. Kim managed to step to the side a little as the zombie attacked her, but still took a nasty blow to the head.

The room started to fill with the smell of burning. Our luck was not getting better. Laura had fallen near an old electric fire that had been on since the Change. As she crashed down onto a coffee table, a few magazines had flown towards the fire and started to smoulder.

"We've got trouble," I said, directing Kim's attention to the smoking magazines.

"All things considered, I think we're due for a break," she cursed, swinging her club at Laura's father.

The magazines started to burn, the flames quickly taking hold and spreading to the carpet. To make matters worse, the zombie blocked my club and pulled it from my grip. The club dropped down the stairs. An instant later, the creature's hand snapped out and had me in a deadly grip. I could feel its cold, dank skin tight against my throat as it tried to choke the life from me. Billy saved the day. His first strike was at the zombie's legs, making it collapse onto its knees – but its grip was so tight I was dragged to the floor with it. I tried to struggle free, but couldn't. Billy's club just missed my face as it whizzed past. It even missed Laura's father, striking the floor uselessly. Judging by the crazed look on Billy's face, he didn't know what he was doing.

"You won't kill me!" Billy was yelling again and again.

My arm was aching – not helped by one of Billy's wild attacks hitting it full on. More blood poured from the wound. I kicked out and the creature's grip loosened for an instant.

"Bat," Kim shouted from across the room, throwing me her rounders bat, just as the creature started to push itself to its feet. I swung it around my head, bringing it down with full force onto the creature. He crumpled, but it took several more strikes to finish it off. I glanced across the living room at Kim, who was already by Laura's side, dragging her unconscious body away from the spreading flames.

"We showed that one," Billy laughed, in a voice I was starting to believe wasn't remotely sane.

"She's okay," Laura said, visibly relieved. "At least I think she's okay. She's not dead, which has to be a good thing, right?"

I was nodding when the baby's cries grew louder and were joined by another sound – zombies. The second zombie in the room had vanished during the fight with Laura's father. It didn't take a genius to work out where it'd gone.

"The baby," we both said at the same time.

"Billy, get everyone out of here. The fire's spreading and we won't be able to stop it."

The insanity left Billy's eyes and was replaced by a cold urge to survive.

"What about Laura?" he asked.

"Get Doug to help and get her out too."

"Don't need help, I'm thirteen," he grumbled, somehow lifting Laura up and wrapping an arm around her. She stirred a little as he did so, then he helped her down the stairs, warning the others of the fire as he went.

"The baby," I whispered.

"We can do this. It's only one zombie. No problem," Kim smiled.

Only it wasn't one zombie, it was two, and they were facing each other. Once in the bedroom, I closed the door to hold the smoke at bay a little while longer.

Nice one, my own voice thought. You're trapped on the top floor of a burning hotel with two zombies and a screaming baby. Way to go.

The one we'd already seen was just to the side of the door, trying to get at the baby in the cot. In between them was the second. A female creature that when alive had been about forty and… I nudged Kim and pointed at a photo of Laura and her parents on the wall. It was Laura's mother. Another zombie that might have been a young chef when it was alive was by her feet, not moving and very, very dead. The baby was crying in his cot, which at the foot of a huge double bed. The two creatures seemed to be growling. At least that's the nearest word to describe the awful, guttural noise they were making. It was the sound of hatred and anger. The sound of living death.

Across the room, two glass doors were open, leading to a

balcony, smoke starting to float out of them. There was a small round table and a couple of chairs there. A cup of tea and some biscuits on the table.

"She's protecting the baby," I whispered, not quite believing what we were witnessing.

The male zombie surged forward, only to be pushed back by Laura's mother. She snarled, like a cornered tiger.

I tried to sneak to the side.

"It's alright," I said, trying to keep my voice as calm as possible. "We're here to save the baby."

She was quick, I'll give her that. Before I'd even finished talking, she backhanded me across the room. Suit Zombie seized his chance and launched himself at Laura's mother, the two creatures crashing onto the floor.

Kim was already at the cot and gently lifted the screaming baby from it. Its mother gave a howl of rage and lifted Suit Zombie from the ground before hurling him towards the balcony, where he landed with a sickening thud. The baby went on crying, and the dead mother turned and started walking towards Kim.

"We can't get out!" Billy screamed from below. "The zombies are here!"

Kim moved to my side as Laura's mother came towards us. Two more zombies entered the room. The mother looked at us and then her baby before turning to roar what sounded like a warning at the two new creatures. They both looked stronger and fresher though.

The battle with the other zombie had left Laura's mother damaged, one arm hanging loosely at her side. Her head looked broken, and her left leg damaged.

She dragged herself past us, attacking the new creatures, or trying her best to. She went down under a flurry of blows, letting out one final cry of rage before giving up the fight. For the first time I felt something like sorrow for one of the creatures.

"The balcony," I said, urging Kim towards the patio doors, as smoke now streamed in under the other door.

I was about to follow her when a hand grabbed my ankle, almost making me fall forward. I looked down to see the broken body of the zombie that had been hurled there – it was still alive, or what passed for life. It was hardly able to move but its eyes still burned with red fury. It was trying to drag itself towards my leg – its jaws open ready to bite me. It never got the chance. Kim instinctively kicked out at it, ending its breathless hunger.

Outside, I quickly tried to close the doors, but the latest corpse had fallen half in the room and half on the balcony, making the doors impossible to shut. From down below I could hear our friends shouting as they left the building, the smoke and flames starting to spread into the rest of the hotel. The door into the bedroom was on fire now.

"So whose stupid plan was this?" Kim laughed, holding the still sobbing baby close.

"Must've been mine," I smiled. "I'm sure you'd have come up with something much better."

The two zombies moved towards us, reaching the patio doors. Inches away from being able to get to us.

"We could jump," Kim said.

"Don't fancy our chances," I said.

"Yeah, 'cause right now they're so good," Kim smiled.

Despite everything, I laughed.

From across the room, the wreck of a creature that had once been Laura's mother roared to her feet. She was a mess, even by zombie standards. Only pure primeval rage was keeping her going. She moved forward quicker than any zombie I'd seen, straight towards the two creatures in front of us. I pulled Kim and the baby to the side – just as Laura's mum charged into the other zombies, forcing all three over the balcony and down to the car park below. One last desperate attack with the last breath of her undead life.

For a moment, we couldn't move. Not really certain what we'd just seen.

"She saved us," Kim whispered.

"No," I said. "She saved the baby. We just got lucky."

I glanced over the balcony. None of the three bodies below were moving.

"Very lucky," I added as Doug and Charlie appeared, carrying a ladder and quickly putting it against the wall.

"The fire's spreading fast," Doug shouted up. "Think it might be a good idea to leave. I suggest you use the ladder."

We didn't need asking twice. Kim went first, carrying the baby to safety. I was halfway down when flames exploded through the balcony doors.

"Everyone got out okay," Doug explained as I reached the ground. Kim was standing by a semi-conscious Laura and her little brother.

"The fire's got out of control," he explained. "We found a

fire extinguisher but it was no use."

"So much for a place of safety," Charlie sighed.

"We should get back to the coach," I said. "It's not safe here."

"Good point," Doug said, passing on the warning.

People started to drift back to the relative safety of the coach. I was about to join them when Doug pulled me to one side, a smile on his face.

"What's so funny?" I asked, feeling tired and beaten.

"We saved the kid, that's something – and I've got a new car."

He opened his hand to reveal a set of car keys.

I looked blank, not sure what he was getting at.

"It's a Jag. An E-Type Jag. Only one of the best cars ever – and it's right over there. Found the keys in the kitchen."

"But we've got the coach."

"I know, but think about it. In the Jag I can scout ahead, check the roads and so on…"

"You know, that's not such a bad idea," I said.

Doug didn't move, just looked at me as though he was waiting for me to give him permission.

"It belonged to Laura's dad," he explained. "So it's not even stealing as she's sort of inherited it."

"It's a good idea," I said. "Sure you can drive it?"

Doug laughed and ran off towards the car, letting out a cry of joy as he did so. Within a few seconds he was in the Jag and revving its engine.

The world was officially insane.

"Alex, Laura's got something she wants to tell you," Kim said at my side.

We were near the coach, the hotel burning brightly behind us. Laura was holding the baby, and for the first time he wasn't crying. Laura looked okay. Well, as okay as anyone could look in the circumstances.

"I just wanted to say thanks," she smiled, looking far younger than she was. "For helping us. You didn't have to and…"

She broke down then and started to cry, tears flowing down her cheeks. Kim went to take the baby but Laura shook her head and managed to stop the tears.

"I'm alright. I have to be alright," she sniffed. "And we'll make sure you get home. You saved my brother and now… now I'll make sure we save your sister. I promise. I owe you that much."

I felt myself choking back tears. Kim smiled reassuringly and slipped her hand into mine.

"Get him!" Kegs cried from nearby.

We looked back at the hotel, where he was facing one of the last zombies, a few other kids with him. This latest one looked like he'd once been a chef. Not that much older than us. Now he was a walking corpse.

"He used to be my boyfriend." I heard Laura scream next to me. "What are you doing?"

Kegs and the kids paused for a minute. Even the zombie appeared momentarily confused.

"Don't just stand there," she yelled. "Get him!"

SEVEN

"Time to go," Doug said, a little later.

For a while we were all hypnotised by the burning hotel. Staring deep into the flames.

"I said we need to go," Doug repeated, directing my attention to the road leading up, where a couple of dead were already walking towards the blaze.

"Okay," I said. "We've got the coach and the Jag. Let's get home."

"One thing," Laura said, catching me up as we walked to the coach, the baby crying for all he was worth.

"I need some supplies," she said.

"We should be home soon," I said.

"No, I mean supplies. For the baby. Nappies and stuff."

"We don't know what the journey's going to be like," Kim said. "And there's a big supermarket on the outskirts of town. Might be an idea to stock up with essentials."

"We'll do a list on the way," I nodded.

"What's up?" Kegs asked, holding Rosie by the hand.

"We're getting supplies," I said.

"Cool," he laughed. "I'm gagging for some chocolate biscuits."

"There it is," Charlie said, pointing to the supermarket.

The coach followed Doug's Jag into the almost empty car park. Luckily for us the Change had happened late on a Friday, after the store had closed.

"Right," I said. "I'll go in with Doug, Charlie and Molly. The rest of you keep an eye open for the dead. Just because we've not seen any for a mile or two doesn't mean they're not still about."

"Like that one there?" Rosie said, pointing to a teenage zombie trapped in the shop part of a petrol station.

"Yeah, just like that one. He can't hurt us though."

"Wouldn't it be better if we all went?" Kegs said. "You won't be able to carry all the bags."

"They'll use trolleys, silly," Rosie explained.

"Fair enough. Well, I'm going to get some shut-eye. Wake me up when you're back."

"Sure you should go?" Kim asked. "Your arm still looks pretty sore."

"It's fine," I lied. "Looks worse than it is."

That part happened to be true. However, it hurt worse than it looked and it looked really bad.

"Pete, any luck with the internet?"

A tired-looking Pete, shook his head, both laptop and phone useless. "I'll give it another five minutes and try later."

"Okay, got the list?"

Charlie nodded.

"Don't forget the biscuits," Kegs shouted out. "And some crisps too."

"So," Molly smiled. "Who's got the keys?"

"I brought a spanner," Charlie said, and then added, "I don't think it's going to be able to smash the glass though."

"We're rubbish thieves," Molly laughed. "Always thought crime would be easier."

"Maybe there's a window we could use?" I suggested, scanning the walls for a way in.

"Where's Doug gone?" Charlie asked, just as we heard the Jag's engine kicking in.

"I think we should move," I suggested, as the car revved its engines a few yards away from us.

We just had time to move out of the way as it shot past us, crashing through the shop's front doors and skidding to a halt just inside, the bonnet buckling and smoking slightly. Doug laughed as an airbag almost smothered him.

"Shop's open," he grinned, climbing out of the car.

"That was really dumb. You could have run us over," I shouted.

For a second, Doug's face changed and I thought he was going to hit me. It was a glimpse of the kid he'd once been. But then he just laughed and apologised.

"Sorry, I should've warned you, but I'm guessing we don't have much time and it was the quickest way to get in."

"He's got a point," Molly said.

"Show-off," Charlie laughed, but I got the feeling he was a little bit jealous of the way Molly had looked at his friend.

"Okay, let's get some trolleys. We shop in pairs," I said.

"Got a pound on you?" Charlie asked.

"What?"

"A pound for the trolleys. They're all chained up to stop kids nicking them."

"I don't think I have any change on me," I said, searching the pockets of my jeans as one of the cash tills crashed to the ground.

"Here," Molly said, picking a couple of pound coins from the smashed till and throwing them towards Doug and myself. "You can pay me back later."

"I know it's pointless but I really have the urge to get a big TV," Doug said. "It's like my brain's still not accepted what's happening."

"My dad would've called this the big shop," I said, as I scanned the aisles for zombies.

"What, crashing a car into a supermarket and taking what you want?"

"No, just doing one huge shopping trip like this. He used to call it the big shop."

"He got that off TV," Doug said. "From that comedian, you know the one who did that sitcom years ago set in the nightclub?"

"Really?"

"Yeah. They just made a new series of it. It's starting next week."

Doug stopped shopping for a moment and looked really sad.

"Only I guess it's not now. Funny ain't it? After everything that's happened that's the thing that really hacks me off."

"For me it's the zombies trying to kill us," I smiled. "Though now that I think about it, I'm going to miss the FA Cup semifinal. My dad had managed to get tickets too."

"Really?" Doug said, impressed.

A tin of baked beans bounced off the shelf to our right.

"What was that?" I asked, only to see Doug grab his shoulder and curse.

"Air rifle," Doug snarled, looking up to the booth that was at the end of the aisle. "Someone's shooting at us. Forgot how much the pellets hurt."

We both moved to the side of the shelves, flattening ourselves against the rows of tinned food.

"Let that be a warning to you!" a kid's voice said over the supermarket's speaker system. "Now get out of my dad's shop!"

I glanced up at the booth to see a gawky-looking kid a few years younger than me taking aim from the smashed glass of the booth. His hair was dark and greasy, flopping over thick black-rimmed glasses.

"We just need some supplies," I said. "We don't mean you any harm."

A can fell off the shelf a little too close to Doug's face for comfort.

"If you shoot me again I'll stick that gun up your..." Doug started to shout.

"Easy," I said, calming my new friend down.

"We're just passing through," I shouted. "You can join us if you want to."

I noticed Molly and Charlie were walking carefully up the staircase leading to the booth, unseen by our attacker. It was risky. If he turned to the side they'd be spotted.

"I'm fine here, thank you very much," the kid yelled down to us. "Now on the way with you, or I'll let the dogs out."

Charlie and Molly froze.

"He's a bloody nutter," Doug whispered.

"You do know what's happened, don't you?" I asked, stepping out into the open with my arms raised.

"Course I do," the kid shouted back. "What do you think I am – some kind of nutter?"

"I'm Alex and this is my friend Doug. Are you okay?"

The kid paused for a moment before replying.

"I'm fine," he said.

"That's good. What are you doing here though? Are you hiding?"

"Don't be daft," he said. "It'd be a rubbish place to hide. I'm here with my parents."

Charlie and Molly screamed as they rushed into the booth. The kid vanished for a moment and Doug and me rushed towards the stairs leading to the booth. By the time we entered the office, the fight was over. Molly was holding the air rifle and grinning, the kid was cringing on the floor in front of her and Charlie was blushing.

"Lucky shot," he mumbled, looking in a bit of pain.

"You should have seen him," Molly grinned. "He was so brave. He threw himself in front of me and took the bullet."

"Did he get hurt?" I asked, concerned. "From this range…"

"No, he… he…" Molly started laughing.

"I got shot in the bum, okay!?" Charlie sulked. "It's not funny."

"It is a bit funny," Molly smiled. "But don't worry, you're still my hero."

Molly smiled and pecked a now blushing Charlie on the lips.

I noticed Doug stopped laughing at the sight of this.

"You okay?" I asked the kid, hoping to change the subject.

"Please don't hurt me," he whimpered.

"We're not going to hurt you," I said, offering a hand to help him to his feet. "We really are just passing through."

The kid allowed me to help him to his feet.

"What's your name?" I asked.

"Kelvin," he answered. "Kelvin Stickley."

"How old are you, Kelvin?" I asked.

"Fourteen and a half," Kelvin replied, which surprised me. He sounded younger. A lot younger.

He was about to say something else when there was a crashing sound beyond the door on the other side of the office.

"Excuse me," he said. "That'll be Mum. She's in a weird mood at the moment. Probably annoyed that I haven't introduced you."

Before any of us could react, Kelvin opened the door and stepped to one side as his mother entered the room.

His zombified mother.

"It's okay," he said. "They're not the bad kids."

Rope was tied around his mother's waist, preventing her getting too far out of the stock room. Something else growled from inside the door and I noticed a male zombie was also there. I could only watch, horrified, as he started to crawl out of the cupboard. Something had damaged his legs and they were useless.

We backed away, Doug raising his bat.

"They're zombies," Molly said, horrified.

"I know," Kelvin replied matter-of-factly. "I think that's why they've been in such a bad mood."

Doug glanced at me and mouthed the words "I told you so."

"It's not safe here," I started to explain, as Kelvin's mum tried and failed to pull herself free of her ropes.

"I'll say," Kelvin answered. "First the shelf-stackers got all weird and then some bad kids turned up. Thought they could help themselves, they did, but Mum and Dad soon chased them away. They'll think twice about shoplifting again, let me tell you."

"Listen to me very carefully," I said, trying to keep the revulsion from my voice. "Your parents aren't your parents anymore. They're dead and they'll kill you if they get the chance."

Kelvin laughed. Doug had been right all along. Whatever horrors Kelvin had witnessed had snapped his mind.

He stopped laughing and glanced at the security monitors lining one wall of the office. A group of four young kids could be seen on one monitor scrambling into the store through the handy hole in the wall Doug had created.

"The cameras are still working," Molly said. "You still have power."

"Course," Kelvin answered. "There's a generator in the cellar. Now, if you'll excuse me, there seem to be some more thieves arriving."

I glanced up at the security screens. Kelvin's mum was looking at them too and staggered forward, pawing the screens trying to reach the small figures on them.

"It's okay," said Kelvin. "They'll learn."

I didn't recognise the kids but they looked young and scared. Turned out the oldest was twelve.

"Get out of my dad's store," Kelvin shouted over the tannoy. "Or I shall be forced to use violence."

"Look!" Molly said. "Behind them – zombies!"

Three or four of the walking dead were following them into the shop. The kids were too busy grabbing food to notice them.

"Shelf-stackers," Kelvin said. "I thought they'd gone home."

"Where's our mates?" Charlie asked.

The next thing happened quickly. Almost too quickly. Molly grabbed the microphone from Kelvin's hand and screamed a warning to the kids below. Surprised, Kelvin staggered backwards – straight into the waiting arms of his mother.

At first glance it looked like she was hugging him – but it soon became clear she was trying to squeeze the life out of him. A growl of hatred was pushed from her mouth as she did so.

Doug reacted instinctively and far quicker than I did. Within a second, he'd pulled Kelvin from his mother's arms and pushed her to the ground.

Kelvin's eyes were wide and terrified, and for a moment I thought our new dreadful reality was starting to gain a foothold in his brain.

Doug brought the bat down once, twice, before Kelvin flung himself in front of my friend and begged him to stop.

Doug didn't seem that concerned. Kelvin, tears flowing freely now, was standing in between my friend and his zombified mother. For her part, she was trying to push herself to her feet, but one of her legs had been damaged in the attack and she no longer seemed able to stand. Just as well, as her son would surely have been killed if she could.

"Don't kill them," Kelvin sobbed. "They're my parents."

Outside our booth, a familiar voice cried out "Geronimo" and I saw on the monitors Kegs, Kim and Billy arriving in the store just in time to save the young kids, taking down the creatures with ruthless efficiency.

"Leave her," I said to Doug. "It should be his call."

Doug seemed thoughtful before nodding and taking a step back.

"I know what they are," Kelvin sobbed. "I know it, but they're still my parents. There has to be something left of them in there. There just has to be."

Kelvin sniffed back his tears and looked up at me.

"I mean, if it was your parents who'd changed what would you do?" he asked.

A shiver went through me. It was a question I didn't want to answer. Not yet. Not ever.

"Listen, we've got to go and we're taking some food. Is there anything you want in return?"

Kelvin shook his head. Both his parents were still straining at their ropes.

"You can come with us, if you want to," I offered.

"I have to stay," he answered. "They need me."

Charlie shook his head and placed an arm around Molly, who had started to cry.

"Everything okay?" Kegs asked, appearing in the doorway of

the office and almost attacking the zombies himself.

"Fine," I said. "We're just leaving."

"What about them?" Kegs asked, looking at Kelvin's parents.

"Leave them. It's Kelvin's call. We'll put a warning outside. Paint it on the wall or something. The rest is up to Kelvin."

"Kid looks a nutter to me," Kegs said, bringing a smile to Doug's face.

"Thank you," Kelvin muttered as we left the strange scene.

As I reached the doorway, I turned back to give him one last warning. "If you give them a chance, they will kill you."

"Do you really reckon it was the right call?" Doug asked, as we finished the shopping.

"No," I replied honestly. "But I didn't like the alternative."

"Me neither," Doug agreed.

He fell silent for a moment before adding, "Sometimes, I hope we never get home."

EIGHT

"Can't believe you forgot the biscuits," Kegs complained for the millionth time since leaving the supermarket. Ahead of us, Doug and the now beaten-up Jag were still leading the way. The Jag had been one of Doug's better ideas. As had a pair of walkie-talkies we'd found in the supermarket. It gave us the chance to stay in touch as Doug acted as our pathfinder, searching for passable roads. Not an easy thing to do when so many cars had been left abandoned – or worse still had crashed as their owners died and changed at the wheel. We had to be quick, too, because the dead were always there, waiting for us. Almost every zombie we passed would remain silent as we sped by, only to start stumbling after us moments later. The four kids we'd picked up in the supermarket were asleep in their seats. They'd been playing computer games at one of their houses when the Change had happened.

Originally there'd been six of them.

We'd picked up other survivors along the way. A group of three ten-year-olds from an abandoned school. Grace, a tough tomboy, was their leader, Mickey and Jane the only other survivors. The three lived nearby and had fled to the school after their own bad times at home. There were a few others. Tasmin and Gertie, twin six-year-olds we nearly missed as they only started running after the coach after we'd passed them, and a group of six kids swerving around in a transit van. The oldest was fourteen and had never had a driving lesson in his life.

Then there was Stacy.

It all went wrong when we stopped to help Stacy.

Remember when your mum used to say don't talk to strangers. Stacy's why. Though like idiots we didn't realise until it was way too late.

We met her a few miles out of town. We were tired and our guards were down. Even after the supermarket we still didn't really think about the way things had... Well, there's a reason these days we call it the Change. It wasn't just the over-eighteens who changed. Case in point. Empty road. Motorway. After spending hours carefully getting out of Dodge, we found what passed for an open road. Okay, so every now and again the car's headlights would catch some zombie at the side of the road (or in the road) and I swear each time we'd jump and then laugh to cover up the fact that we'd just jumped. I was in the Jag with Doug. We were making good time and about to pass Leeds when we saw a girl running from a couple of deadbeats straight into our path.

"It's a girl," Doug said, skidding the Jag into the first zombie (a fat bloke with bad teeth) before I even knew what was happening. He was out of the car in an instant and took care of the second zombie – a deadbeat who looked like a student. By the time I'd got out of the car, Doug was already chatting to the new girl.

"Oh, thank you," she almost swooned, putting both arms around a very startled Doug, who didn't seem to mind that much.

"I thought I'd had it for sure that time," she said, choking back a sob.

"Well, you're safe now," Doug smiled, looking more than a little bit flustered.

The new girl, who quickly told us her name and that she was all on her own, was about our age and very pretty. Dark black hair cut into a short bob, a little too much make-up for me, but that didn't seem to bother Doug.

"Yeah," Charlie said, joining them. "But I don't think we should hang about."

We looked to the side of the road, where an old pub still had a few punters inside. Dead punters who were starting to wonder what all the commotion was.

"Think the pub must be short on bar snacks," Doug said. Stacy laughed a little too much.

"Where are you heading?" she asked, glancing around nervously. "Somewhere safe?"

"Nowhere's safe these days," Doug answered.

I'm sure he was talking a bit lower than normal, as if he was trying to sound a little older.

"We're heading home. There's a TA Centre in St Helens. Should be safe there."

"Ah," the girl said, sounding a little disappointed. "How are you going to get past Leeds?"

It was a good question and one that had worried us all along the way. Leeds was a city and cities were full of people and lots of people meant… well, I'm sure you can do the maths.

"Only some mates are holed up in a yard on the outskirts of town. It's about as safe as you can get now. Sure they wouldn't mind you crashing the night there," Stacy said.

"Cool," Doug grinned. "That's just what we need."

And you know the worst thing, we all agreed with him.

Idiots.

It went down like this.

For a while (all of five minutes or so), we liked her. Hey, she was seventeen, cool and pretty. So shoot us.

So we listened to her and we followed her through the outskirts of Leeds because, and I quote: "Trust me, you don't want to stay on the main road. It gets worse just past the city centre. A lot worse."

And we trusted her because – and despite everything I still hold to this – if you can't trust people, if you can't at least give them the benefit of the doubt, we truly are all doomed.

So for a while, her shortcut was great. Almost empty roads and not that many zombies.

"The yard's just there," she explained.

We'd been driving through an industrial part of the city, lots of empty warehouses waiting to be demolished or converted into new flats. A few had already been altered opposite the yard but had no signs of life in them.

"Better stop for a sec. My mates might be a bit jumpy," she said, leaping out of the Jag. I'd somehow ended up on the back seat so she could direct Doug. She ran up to the gates and banged her fist against them. A steel shutter opened up and for a few seconds she seemed to be arguing with someone on the other side. We couldn't make out the words clearly but it looked quite emotional.

Normally it might have set my spider sense off, but remember none of us had slept properly for over twenty-four hours by this point. Tired does not describe the state we were in.

"Sorry," Stacy said as she climbed back into the car. The gates started to open in front of us. "They took a bit of convincing. Fine now, though."

We drove through the gates, about half a dozen kids lining the sides to watch us enter. They looked like they'd lived wild all their lives, their clothes torn and stained. The gates closed behind us.

"I'm sorry," Stacy said. "I really am. But I have to help him. I have to."

"What do you mean?" I asked, as the first of my friends started to get out of the coach.

"Hold on," Doug said, sounding suspicious. "That kid's got a gun."

"Stacy…" I started to say, only to see her hit Doug on the back of the head.

"What have you done?" I yelled. "You've killed him."

"No," she sobbed. "No. I've not. He's just unconscious. I promise."

"Stacy, what's going on?" Molly shouted, jogging towards the car, Kim and Kegs close behind.

"I should think that's obvious, ain't it?" a ferret-faced skinhead of about seventeen said. "We're robbing you."

More kids appeared out of nowhere (well, thinking back it was out of the warehouses at either side of us, but at the time it felt like nowhere) as I hurriedly climbed out of the car. There must have been about thirty. Only a few looked as vicious as Ferret Face, but it was enough to make me realise we were in real trouble.

They didn't look like normal kids. I know that probably sounds stupid, but I remember thinking at the time they looked more like a pack of feral cats than kids.

"Don't be stupid," Molly said.

Ferret Face backhanded Molly to the ground.

I rushed towards him and there it was, staring straight in my face.

The gun.

My blood froze and, well, you've heard all the clichés and I tell you what, they're all true. I was so scared I couldn't move, and my heart was hammering so loud I could've sworn everyone could hear its frantic beating.

"Not so brave now, are you?" Ferret Face grinned.

He was laughing and sweating and, even though I have no experience of it, I could've sworn he was on something.

"Jacko, don't hurt them," Stacy cried out. "You promised."

"Pow!" he yelled, his laughter reminding me a little of the Joker.

Which was fine if I'd been Batman. Problem was I didn't even have the moves to be Robin.

"That could have been the gun going off," he cackled, ignoring Stacy's pleas. "This one here. With bullets in and everything. That could've been you. Now get everyone off the coach, nice and slowly. No, make that nice and quickly or I'll blow your brains out."

"Listen," Kim said. "There's no need for this. We can help each other."

Boom!

Now, I don't know if you've ever heard a gun going off but it's not a sound you ever forget. It's loud and it's scary and the sound happens so quick you worry you might have been shot.

"The next one doesn't go into the air," he warned us.

Kim nodded. For a second, I thought she was going to faint. I know I nearly did.

"And you, get away from her!" he yelled, waving the gun at Charlie, who was on one knee by the semi-stunned Molly.

"Ease up, mate," Charlie smiled, trying his best to sound friendly. "I'm just checking she's okay."

They were his last words. Ferret Face fired again, this time hitting Charlie straight in his chest.

There was blood. A lot of blood. A few of us screamed. A few of their gang too, but even more just laughed and urged him on as he fired again. This one finished the job. They were animals. I don't know what they had gone through and I don't care. I wish I could forget but I can't. I can't forget my friend's body twitching and convulsing as the life left him. I can't forget Molly's desperate, heartbreaking sobs by his side. And I'll never forget the whoops of laughter and cheers from those kids. Only Stacy wasn't laughing and cheering. She was pale and shocked.

Molly was trying to stem the flow of blood with just her hands but we could all see it was pointless. It was obvious Charlie was done for the moment the first shot was fired. Eventually, after what seemed like hours but was less than a minute, he gave one last terrifying gasp and stopped moving. His red shirt darkening with his own blood.

"Jacko Glover strikes again!" Ferret Face laughed. "That was the best one yet. Now get everyone off the coach or I kill you. Them. Everyone. And I still take the coach."

People started to file off the coach, some crying, others too shell-shocked to do even that.

"Ah, is lil' baby all upset?" Glover mocked as I realised I had tears coming down my cheeks as well.

"I know what you're thinking, punk," he said, putting on a very bad American accent. "You're wondering if you can take me out before I shoot you. So I guess you got to ask yourself if you're feeling lucky. So are you, punk? Are you feeling lucky?"

I didn't move.

Glover burst out laughing.

"That's my Clint Eastwood impression. You know, from that film he did."

He glanced around the yard. "Everyone off the coach? Good. Let's get out of here."

"Mack, you sure you can drive this thing?" he asked some kid about his own age, as his gang started to file onto the coach.

The kid nodded but didn't look him in the eye.

"Okay, Stacy and Malcolm. You've got the car. The rest in the coach. Someone get the gates open. We're moving out."

The doors opened to reveal four or five zombies standing

there, waiting to get in. One of the kids opening the gates was attacked straight away and died within seconds. The other made it to the coach.

"Oh well," Glover said, looking down at the latest corpse. "You win some, you lose some."

The coach started to move slowly forward.

"You're welcome to this place," he shouted out, hanging onto the coach as he stood in the doorway to yell at us. "But I don't think you'll like the neighbours much."

And with that the coach turned the corner and was gone.

I glanced around the yard. Everyone looked as shocked as me, their minds racing to try and process what had just happened. Molly was still holding Charlie's body, Kim trying to comfort her. Matt was lying against an old dustbin, his leg obviously causing him a great deal of pain.

"Where's Chris and Rosie?" I asked.

Kegs cursed under his breath.

"I told them to hide," he said, looking scared for the first time. "I told them to hide and not come out until I said it was safe. They're still on the coach."

NINE

For one terrible moment no one moved. The only sounds were the cries coming from Laura's baby brother.

And then two things happened almost instantly.

Billy said "Zombies", and Doug started to regain consciousness. Billy's word pulled us all back to Earth just as half a dozen dead were shambling their way through the open gates to the yard – with others behind them. Looking back, I can't remember stopping them. I have vague memories of stepping forward with Kegs and then the creatures weren't a problem.

"Charlie?" Doug's voice sounded a little broken.

"They killed him," Molly sobbed. "Stacy led us into a trap and they just shot him. How could they do that? How?"

"Where's the coach?" Doug asked.

"They took it," I said, directing a couple of kids to close the gates.

Doug squatted by Charlie's body and closed his dead friend's eyes.

"I'm sorry," he whispered.

When Doug rose to his feet and talked to me, I didn't recognise him.

"Which way did they go?" he asked, in a voice that reminded

me of distant thunder.

"Left," Billy said. "And they have the kids."

"Not for long," Doug said, walking towards the gate. "Kegs?"

"We'll need a car," Kegs said, picking up a crowbar from a pile of tools left scattered at the side of the yard.

"Shouldn't we stick together?" a young kid asked.

Looking back, I think they were more worried about two of our toughest kids running off and not coming back.

"They killed Charlie," Doug said, as if that answered all the kid's concerns.

"And they have Chris and Rosie," I added, though looking at Doug's face, I was fairly certain he only had one thing on his mind.

"And we need the coach back," Molly said, joining us and wiping tears away. "Charlie would have wanted us to be safe."

"You okay?" I asked.

"No. You?"

I shook my head. "Not remotely."

As we reached the partially closed gate I paused and looked back at the others.

"Close the gate. Open it for no one but us. And check the surrounding buildings. Make sure it's safe. If they were staying here it should be, but you never know. We'll be back soon."

Two zombies were approaching. I was still a few yards behind Doug and Kegs, looking back at my other friends, some concerned, most worried as the huge solid steel gates were pulled together.

"Zombies," I warned.

Doug took them out without a second thought, striding away

from the yard to a converted warehouse nearby.

"Flats?" Kegs asked.

Doug nodded.

I was confused, shocked and becoming acutely aware of how it was already starting to get dark again. Without the streetlights working, twilight seemed far more dangerous. Just not as dangerous as Doug.

Kegs used the crowbar to smash the glass in the front door of the entrance hall to the block of flats. I think the area must've been some kind of rejuvenation zone where they were converting old warehouses into smart new homes.

After smashing the glass, Kegs opened the door, looking around furtively as he did so. I wasn't sure if he was on the lookout for zombies or police.

Inside was quiet and normal. No sign of the dead. Kegs and Doug started to walk slowly up the staircase. Something had just changed, and now Kegs was acting like Doug's partner. I followed them with Molly, feeling a little like a hanger-on.

"I thought the cars would be underneath the flats," I said.

"They are," Kegs answered. "But we need keys first."

Doug shushed us as we reached the first floor, and put the side of his head to one of the doors to listen.

After a few seconds, he raised three fingers to indicate how many zombies he thought were waiting and beckoned Kegs towards the door.

Kegs used the crowbar on the lock and kicked the door open, smacking a zombie in the head almost straight after.

"More of them!" I said from behind, but I needn't have worried. By the time I'd finished speaking Doug and Kegs had taken care of them. I know both had been in the TA, apparently as a way of straightening them out, and you could see a bit of military precision in the way they were approaching things.

Doug squatted down by one of the corpses, quickly searching the dead man's pockets. It looked like a young couple had lived in the flat before the Change and that a friend had been over just before…

Kegs made for the kitchen. Doug pulled out a wallet filled with money and laughed out loud (with more than a touch of bitterness it seemed to me), tossing it to one side.

"Got 'em," Kegs said from the kitchen doorway.

"What do you reckon?" Doug asked. "Couple more just to be safe?"

Kegs nodded.

The next flat was empty, leading both to curse. The third was the jackpot. Kegs opened the door using the same method as last time – only this time, instead of finding a couple of zombies waiting for us in the flat's entrance hall, we found eight – all in fancy dress!

I was ready to run away when Kegs and Doug both looked at each other and nodded.

"Geronimo!" Kegs yelled, diving into the mass of zombies.

Doug took two out straight away. They pushed the dead beyond the doorway to what was the living room, allowing me to follow them in. I nearly tripped over one of the bodies and soon found myself pinned against the wall by a dead guy who had come to the party dressed as some kind of giant bumblebee. I tried bringing my club around but couldn't get a good strike. I was starting to find it hard to breathe when Molly came to my rescue. She was screaming and crying and yelling, bringing a chair leg down again and again on the bee until there wasn't much of it left.

"Thanks," I spluttered, getting my breath back.

She was still crying and staring down at the dead bee.

"Be careful," I said to Molly, following Kegs into the living room.

By this point most of them were already beaten, but Kegs was struggling with a zombie police officer. I ducked a swinging arm from a zombie Wolverine and took him out with a backswing of my club before bringing it down onto the one attacking Kegs. It took two strokes to stop him and, by the time a relieved-looking Kegs rolled out from underneath the latest body, the fighting was over, Doug stepping into the living room.

"Wuss," he called over to Kegs, who was rubbing his red neck.

"Caught me by surprise, that's all," Kegs answered, accepting my offer to help him to his feet.

A quick check for more zombies revealed none but did help us to find a pile of coats, jackets and handbags – most with car keys inside.

"Result," Doug said. "Now we can go to the garage."

It didn't take us long to find a car. One of the party-goers had a jeep. A jeep! I mean, who has a jeep in the middle of a city?

Doug had changed. I mean, we all had, but there was a cold craziness about him now that was really scary and made Kegs appear like an innocent little kid.

"Watch this," Doug said, as we shot out of the garage, our brakes screeching as we turned and carried on down the road – in the opposite direction to which the coach had gone. Four or five zombies were already outside the yard gate, banging at it with their dead fists as though they expected my friends to let them in.

"What are you doing?" I asked.

"Live and learn," he replied, putting his foot on the brakes and spinning the car round to face the other way. He revved the engine and took off, zooming down the street and mowing down the zombies.

"Should slow them down for a while," he said. "Now, let's get our coach back."

We followed the road, looking for signs of the thieves, only there weren't any. There was just a dead city and a dead world. Ilkley had been bad but Leeds was far, far worse. The outskirts were full of buildings half burnt down. Quite a few had collapsed and were now merely smouldering ruins. The fires were a stroke of luck, as they helped illuminate our way and made it easier to avoid the burnt-out cars and junk scattered in the road. We passed a lot of dead bodies too. Some dead dead and others still walking. Occasionally a zombie would stop and just watch us drive by, the fire from a nearby building flickering eerily in their dead eyes. After an hour, Kegs and Doug fell into a morose silence. I was in the back seat with Molly and had the ridiculous feeling that it was just like when I was a kid with my sister in the back of my parents' car. Occasionally our headlights would hit on a startled kid. Most ran away – madness and death in their eyes. Another gang pelted us with stones and bottles – trying to steal our ride I guess – so we drove on. Always in our vision were some of the main blocks of the city centre. Some burnt-out shells and wrecks, others still burning like beacons in the night. I tried not to think about all the death, but couldn't help it. The scale of the whole disaster was starting to hit home.

"It really is all dead," I mumbled from the back, as we risked a quick trip through the centre. It was even worse close up. The fires had spread through a lot of the city, row after row of burnt-out shops passed to either side of us.

… And then, when we were about to give up and head back, we saw it.

The coach.

And, get this, it was parked outside one of the few rows of shops untouched by the fires and Glover and his gang were loading it up with boxes of stolen goods. The Jag was nearby. Kids were taking TVs and music equipment out of a nearby shop. As we watched, one of them dropped a bag and it fell open, money scattering on the wind.

The gang had broken through a set of gates to gain access to an arcade of upmarket shops. Some of the crew waited on each side of the coach, keeping watch for zombies and taking them out when any approached. Already ten or so bodies could be seen lying motionless near them. Glover was obviously running things, waving the gun around in the air. Doug had stopped the jeep a safe distance away so we could watch proceedings without being seen, ignoring a couple of approaching zombies.

"Let's get 'em," Kegs said.

Doug didn't say anything but carried on watching the gang as they loaded the coach with the goods.

"You know," he said, after a few minutes' silence. "I think they might be the most stupid kids I've ever actually seen. All this and they're stealing."

There was a tapping at the window by my side and I jumped. A thin, dark-haired woman in her forties (or at least she had been in her forties before she'd died and come back to life as a rotting bag of flesh and bone) was standing there, banging the back of her hand against the window. For a moment, she seemed to be confused but then started to get angry – probably around the time she realised we were still alive.

I gripped my golf club and brought it up in front of me. Doug turned round and smiled – it wasn't one of those good smiles either.

"Got it," he said, starting the car's engine and backing it away from the gang slowly, making sure they didn't see us. He turned the corner and stopped, allowing the zombies time to catch us up before starting it up again. A few more of the dead staggered out of the shadows. He drove to the end of the road, passing a burnt-out cinema and stopping just short of the other side of the arcade, where the gate was still closed. I glanced out of the back window. Madwoman was still following us and had been joined by about twenty others. All less than fifty yards away.

"Here's the plan. You open the other gate and let the zombies in. While the gang are distracted, we get the coach and kids and give them a little payback."

"But that's…" I started to say.

"Dangerous?" he finished. "Yeah, it is. I'd ask Kegs but I'll need him for the fight and Molly needs to drive the coach."

Kegs handed me the crowbar and showed me the gate, calmly

ignoring the fact that the zombies were getting closer by the second.

"Old gates," he said. "Chain and padlock. This should deal with it."

"Good luck," Molly smiled, as the jeep pulled away.

I was alone with only the dead for company.

And I'll tell you something, squatting by the gate, sweating despite the cold night air, hands shaking, zombies getting closer and closer – it all added a whole new level to my fear. I risked a glance at the dead. They were less than ten yards away. No sign of Doug or the jeep either. Maybe he'd lied, I thought. Maybe the real plan was for me to cause a distraction by getting torn apart by the zombies. The zombies had been joined by a few of their mates and now numbered around thirty or maybe even forty. It was hard to tell with all the flickering shadows. The zombies themselves were in a far worse state than any others I'd seen. Some had survived the inferno and explosions – or even been caught up in fires after they'd changed. Some dragged broken legs behind them. A few were even missing limbs, oblivious to the grotesque wounds on their decomposing frames.

The crowbar slipped from my hand and clattered to the floor. I was running out of time. Doug was counting on me. Rosie and Chris were counting on me. I started to get angry with myself. Something kicked a can behind me and I turned to see Madwoman was virtually next to me now, her arms outstretched. I was dead. She started to growl or groan or whatever the name is for that horrible grave-like sound they make. I was almost crying with fear as I picked up the crowbar and brought it down angrily on the lock – only to see something truly unbelievable.

It wasn't locked.

All the time I'd been trying to break a link in the chain, the padlock had been there, the bolt open. Whoever had locked the gate hadn't double-checked it. I laughed out loud and pulled it through the chain – just as the woman's cold hand grabbed my shoulder. I turned my head in time to see her other arm coming towards me. I rolled back, her hand passing over me (and if it had hit me, I truly believe it would've taken my head clean off). I tried to scramble away but her miss unbalanced her and she fell forward – landing right on top of me. Her friends were close behind. I kicked out at the gate and it budged a little, but not enough. It also made a noise. A lot of noise. So much noise that the zombies stopped and looked at it. Even Madwoman stopped trying to strangle me to see where the noise had come from. I seized my chance and rolled over, finding myself on top of her. She tried to bite me but missed. Her grip loosened and I managed to shake her off, pushing myself quickly to my feet. The zombies were all around now, their arms stretching out towards me. Some were at the gates, trying to shake them open so they could get to the would-be-thieves at the other end, who now seemed to be the zombies' main focus.

"Come on!" I screamed, losing it quite badly.

I pulled one of the gates back, only a hair's breadth away from the zombies' outstretched, grabbing arms. "Come and get them – dinner is served!"

There was a scream and a bang. One of the dead, dressed as a butcher, suddenly had a hole in him. For a second, it didn't click what it was, and then there was another bang and he had another hole in him and I looked back to see Glover had seen us and was shooting wildly. A third shot hit the butcher in his dead right hand. He looked at the wound, confused. I had the feeling that he was trying to work out what was going on. Something inside him was saying it should hurt and he started to growl furiously, waving his arms about like a mad gorilla. One of the arms caught me and sent me flying back into the shadowed doorway of a nearby shop. I shook my head and was about to get up when I heard shouting and noticed more of the zombies flooding past me. There were far more than twenty now. More like fifty, staggering down towards the screaming gang at the other end of the parade. The kids didn't stand a chance.

It hit me then.

Charlie, the tiredness, the knowledge of how close my own death was, and most of all my worry about Gabs. Tired and alone and broken, I felt certain she was dead, and even if she wasn't there was no way I would ever be able to make it back home to save her. I started to shake uncontrollably. My heart was beating so hard and so fast I was sure it was about to burst out of my chest.

I didn't hear the gunshots and the screams cease. I didn't even hear the sound of a coach starting up.

I was gone.

Terrified.

Lost.

And then there was a hand in the darkness and Doug was pulling me to my feet.

"Come on," he said. "You almost missed the best bit."

TEN

The fight – or what had passed for the fight – had gone like this. When they left me, the others drove back – this time making sure the zombies didn't follow – and sat in the shadows by the side of a building, all the lights off. A lion stalking its prey. They waited and waited until they saw the kids starting to scream and Glover starting to fire madly at yours truly. They pulled the jeep up by the side of the coach and calmly got out. A few kids turned and shouted an alarm, but Doug's timing had been perfect. There were only two of them on the coach and they didn't put up much of a fight. Kegs and Doug didn't kill them. Doug just looked at the two kids and said, "Your friend killed my best mate. You have five seconds to get off the coach."

They scrambled to their feet and ran down the street as fast as they could. The first made it about four or five yards before one of the dead got him. His friend managed to make it all the way to the end of the street before a grasping hand tripped him up. Grey figures appeared out of the shadows. His screams didn't last for long.

"We should get Alex and get out of here," Molly said.

And that was when Doug came back for me.

Doug's plan had worked. Or so we thought. There was just

one minor problem with it.

Rosie and Chris weren't on the coach.

Out of the thirty or so kids who'd attacked us, about ten were left – the rest had fled into the night. Glover had been one of the first to flee – losing his courage when Doug took the gun from him.

The gates to the arcade had been closed again but the zombies were still inside and desperate to get to us. Dead arms were stretching out hungrily through the bars, inches away from where Kegs had made the surviving gang members kneel.

"What happened to the kids?" Kegs asked.

No one answered.

Doug grabbed one and dragged him towards the gate, the zombies becoming more animated as they approached.

"Okay, okay, I'll tell you," the kid cried out, tears flowing down his face.

Doug loosened his grip, the kid scrambling away – looking more scared of Doug than the zombies.

"There was a fight," he whimpered. "Just after we found them."

Kegs went pale.

"What kind of fight?"

"An argument between Stacy and Jacko."

We both looked at the kid, trying to work out who Jacko was.

"Jacko," he said, as though we should all know that. "Our leader. Stacy must've found the kids when she went to the back seat, but she didn't tell anyone. But then when we got here, Jacko found out and wanted to kick them off the coach. Stacy wouldn't let him. They started shouting at each other and then Stacy barged past Jacko with the kids and run off. Jacko warned us not to follow. That she was out of the gang…"

"Which way did they run?" Kegs asked.

The kid turned and looked at the arcade.

"In there," he said.

One of the things life's taught me: Sometimes it goes wrong. And sometimes it *all* goes wrong.

Case in point.

"We've got company!" Molly shouted from the driving seat of the coach.

The coach's headlights shone down the ruined street, illuminating dark and angry shapes rising to their feet and staggering towards us. To my left was the gate to the arcade, where more zombies were trying to reach us, their arms snaking out through the gaps in the gate.

I could hear a voice, my own voice, yelling in my mind, telling me to get a grip, but I wasn't listening.

"Look!" yelled Molly, pointing up the arcade. It was almost black there, but as we looked we saw a torch flashing towards us and, just behind the torch – Christopher.

"Clever kid," Kegs said. "He knows if he shouts the zombies will hear him. Okay, we need to sort this. Molly, get the coach back to the others. We'll take the Jag."

"What about these lot?" Kegs said.

"We should kill them," Doug said.

A few of the kids started whimpering, others cursed.

"We're not killers," I said.

"Charlie's dead," Doug yelled. "They deserve to die."

"They deserve a lot but not that. You knew Charlie better than me, but from what little I knew of him I bet he wouldn't want you to do this. He'd have told you it was wrong."

Doug screamed and fired the gun into the air.

"Get out of here," he said to the gang. "Before I change my mind."

They didn't need to be asked twice.

He looked at the gun as it was the most hateful thing he'd ever seen and hurled it away with a curse.

"Let's get the kids," he said.

Once round the back of the shops, Kegs got straight out of the car, crowbar in hand, sliding the gate back open with ease. The three of us ran down the arcade towards where the torchlight had been seen. The dead spotted us straight away and started to turn. The light was coming from a shop selling African artefacts.

"Go get them, we'll slow the deadheads down," Kegs said.

There was no time to argue. I went into the shop, and to be honest I'm still not completely sure what happened next.

I do know that Glover was waiting for me. His fist shot out. I rolled with the punch at the last instant. It hurt like mad and sent me flying against a shelving unit filled with African carvings. The shelves tipped back and I went with them. Blood was coming from my cut lip and pain lanced through the wound on my arm. Glover started to laugh and bounced around like a boxer in the ring.

"I was going to run off but then I thought, 'No, Jacko, you can't run. You've got unfinished business with the kids who wrecked your crew,' and I was right. So here I am. Just the two of us."

I glanced across the room. Rosie and Chris were there, hugging a beaten and terrified-looking Stacy.

"Oh yeah, and them," he laughed. "But they'll be dead soon so they don't count. Come on then. Let's go."

"You want a fight?" I asked, pushing myself to my feet. "With zombies outside, the world in ruins and our friends in danger – you want to actually have a fight?"

"Yeah," he said. "What's up – you soft or something?"

"Listen, this is pointless. I just want to get the kids to safety…"

He rushed me, hitting me hard in the midriff and sending me crashing against a wall, tribal masks clattering down around me.

Blow after blow rained down and all I could hear was his insane and mocking laughter.

"Leave him alone!" a young voice cried out from behind him, and I was horrified to see Rosie rushing towards him in a brave and stupid attempt to help me.

Glover's right arm snapped back and struck Rosie, sending her flying off her feet and into the counter.

For one terrifying moment I thought he'd killed her, but he

hadn't. Rosie got to her feet and looked like she was going to jump in again. Looking meaner and cooler than any six-year-old had the right to.

"It's okay, Rosie," I smiled, pushing myself up. "I've got this."

Now I'd love to tell you what happened next. To describe each glorious blow, but I can't. The next thing I remember is Doug and Kegs dragging me off a beaten and bruised Glover, telling me he'd had enough.

Rosie and Chris were looking at me with the fear they had when looking at zombies. Hardly surprising – when I caught my dark reflection in the mirror, it made me shiver. With the torchlight the only illumination, I looked like a zombie myself. I hadn't caught sight of myself since before the Change. I looked thinner, haunted and now had Glover's blood on my fists. Kegs and Doug seemed to think I'd done a good thing but, looking down at Glover, I just felt bad, really bad, for what I'd done.

I glanced back to see the door to the shop closed and dark shadows banging against the windows...

"We've got a problem," Doug said. "Way out's blocked."

He and Kegs started talking urgently, while I glanced around the room. Glover was still curled up on the floor, whimpering and murmuring to himself. Rosie was trying to get Kegs' attention, but he was too busy with Doug to notice.

"Excuse me," she said to me. "But they're being silly. If we need to get out, why don't we go out the back way? That's how he got in."

Doug and Kegs heard this and started to laugh. Right on cue, the hammering on the door started to get louder. I grabbed the torch and shone it at the glass. It was like the first day of the sales – only we were the ones on special offer. There must've been at least fifty of the dead out there, all pressing against the windows, trying to get in.

"I think we should go," I said.

"Good plan," Kegs answered. "And don't worry about the fight. He had it coming."

"And more," Doug added.

Rosie tugged at Kegs' shirt, whispering something to him. He looked grim but nodded, allowing Rosie to run back to Stacy.

"If you want, you can come with us. At least until we get out of the city."

Stacy shook her head and shuffled over to the trembling and broken Glover.

"I can't leave him," she said. "He's my brother."

I still remember that, and feeling even sadder for what had happened. It didn't seem to bother Doug and Kegs, but to me, it all seemed messed up. Charlie's death, the fighting...

"How are we going to get back to the car?" I asked.

Right on cue a familiar voice came from Rosie's jacket.

"I think it's for you," she smiled, handing me the walkie-talkie from the car. "Thought it might be fun to have so I borrowed it."

"Alex, are you there?" Molly's voice crackled.

"Yeah, we're here and we need your help. Big time."

"That's what I thought. The creatures are everywhere. You got the kids?"

"Yeah," I said, walking towards the fire exit at the back of the shop. "Can you get to the back doors on the left side?"

"Roger that. Everyone okay?" she asked.

"Yeah, everyone's okay." I paused to look back at Stacy and her brother and added, "Well, pretty much okay."

Just before we left, Rosie ran back into the shop. Worried, we followed her, only to see her peck Stacy on the cheek.

"Thank you for saving me and Christopher," she said, before rushing back to us.

A couple of zombies had discovered the fire exit, but they didn't last long. Just as we got through the door, we heard the windows crash in… then we were on the main road and the coach was there and we were safe.

At least for a little while.

ELEVEN

By the time we got back to the yard, it was nearly two in the morning and we were all completely exhausted. Kegs had fallen asleep on the back seat, the kids holding on to him like a lifebelt (which to them I guess he was), while Doug and myself stayed silent. I didn't have much to say. The blood had dried on my hands now but it still reminded me of how I'd lost it. Doug had told me not to worry about it – that there was no other way – and I knew he was right. I just didn't feel happy about it.

The truth of it was I was tired and pretty close to broken and just wanted to go home to my own bed and curl up until it all went away. Only I couldn't. There was no going home for any of us. At least to the homes we'd once known.

After all we'd been through, I tried not to think about what my sister was going through – if she was still alive.

No, she had to be alive, I'd remind myself almost constantly. She just had to be.

And all the time as I was thinking this, I'd stare out of the coach's window into the nightmarish darkness of a dead city's streets. I saw corpses dragging themselves from shadow to shadow, furtive kids hiding and scurrying through the devastated streets trying their best to survive. Too scared to ask us for help

— or too wary.

The city was as dead as those it now belonged to.

Billy and Kim were standing guard as we returned. There were a number of zombie corpses outside the gate, and it turned out the others had had their own adventure while we were gone. Everyone looked pretty much done in. Most had been asleep in a small warehouse they'd found off the yard as our car pulled in, but soon woke to see if we'd been successful.

"We went shopping," Kim explained, as our friends came out to greet us. The gates behind us were closing tight, a couple more zombies already heading towards them, attracted by the lights and noise. "We needed some clothes badly and noticed you'd got your car from the flats…" Her voice trailed off as she noticed the blood on my fists and the haunted look in my eyes.

I only found out later that Kim, Pete and a few others had gone into the flats, getting clothing and bedding for everyone… and some soap and towels. The basics we were all starting to forget about. Billy had nearly died again – Lizzie saving him this time.

Kim looked older. I wasn't sure if it was the combat trousers and sweatshirt she was now wearing or recent events.

"You okay?" she asked me.

It was dark, the coach's headlights and the full moon our only illumination, but it was enough to see Charlie's body. It had been moved to the side of the yard and a blanket placed over it.

I didn't reply, but just stared for a while at the body of my friend.

"Come with me," Kim whispered, leading me by the hand to a sink they'd found in the yard's makeshift kitchen. Once there she helped me to wash the blood from my hands.

And I know that might sound weird but I was still not really there. Everything had caught up with me and left me… fractured.

After washing the blood away, Kim led me to the part of the warehouse everyone had turned into a makeshift camp.

"You're going to be okay," she whispered again and again. "You're going to be okay."

She gently pushed me against a wall, making me sit down, before covering me with a blanket and pulling me close to her. We stayed that way for a while, Kim slowly rocking me like I was a small child, telling me again and again that everything was going to be okay, until I drifted off into the deepest sleep of my life.

And you know, this might sound soft, but if you've lived through what I have you'll also know how hard it can hit you and you'll understand just how important moments like that are. And I swear in that moment, when Kim softly kissed my forehead and stroked my hair, I think she saved my life.

I really do.

The next day we said goodbye to Charlie. I woke up feeling stronger and more together than I had since before the Change. Something had happened during the night, while I slept. Something small and important. Kim felt it too. We didn't talk about it, but it was there nonetheless. We held hands while talking with the others about Charlie and what to do with him. We couldn't take him with us but we also couldn't leave him behind. At least not the way he was. In the end Doug decided for us when he explained how Charlie had been a fan of Viking history and the old Conan movies. In the first Conan film his girlfriend had died and Conan had cremated her on top of a funeral pyre. Now that might seem weird to you but to us, there and then, it seemed to make perfect sense. We spent the morning scavenging for wood and paper – easy to do as the yard turned out to be an old scrapyard – and by noon we had a funeral pyre built in the centre, Charlie's body resting on top of it. We all stood around it and some of us said a few words. Mine weren't that great. I didn't know Charlie that well but felt like I did. So did everyone. In the two days since the Change, he'd become more than a passing acquaintance from school.

"He was my mate," Doug said, quietly at first but his voice growing in passion as he spoke. I got the feeling he'd been proud to know Charlie. That he was saying goodbye to someone who was far more than just a friend. "When I came to this school I didn't have any mates. Most of you probably still don't know this but I… I'd been pretty wild at my last school and got kicked out. I wasn't a good person, I stole and lied and got into fights. Lots of fights. I even got sent to jail for a while. Kids' jail but still jail. When I got out, Campion was one of the few places that would give me a chance. At first I hated it. I found myself sitting next to Charlie and he was everything I wasn't. He had good folks, a good family and lots and lots of comics and books and films."

A few people laughed at this. People had liked Charlie.

"At first I thought he was the biggest geek I'd ever met in

my life. And he was. But I also thought he was a loser and I was totally wrong about that. For reasons I still can't work out we became mates and he helped me to see things differently. He made me realise that I could be different and now... he's my friend and he's dead and that hurts. That hurts more than anything I've ever known."

Doug paused for a moment. We were all silent. Even the chaos outside seemed to fall silent.

"You know he also loved his music. All the loud stuff especially. Couldn't stand it myself but, like his gran used to say, we were chalk and cheese. So there was this band he liked called Linkin Park and there was this song of theirs called "In the End" that even I liked and Charlie totally loved. The lyrics were something like 'I tried so hard, I tried my best, but in the end it doesn't really matter'... Well, I don't want to argue with Charlie's favourite band but I think in the end it does really matter. What we do, what we say, who we touch. Charlie helped me more than he'll ever know. I think we all loved him a bit too and I think in the end that's all that really matters..."

Doug lit the pyre, and I guess we'd put a little too much petrol on it because the flames whooshed up straight into the darkness, like a massive firework shooting off into the night sky.

And we all started to clap and cheer and shout Charlie's name.

And I know this probably sounds really crazy – especially as I don't believe in much these days – but I like to think we cheered and clapped Charlie all the way to Heaven and somehow he was looking down on us all and laughing his head off.

Sorry. I'm going to have stop for a while. It's just... well, you know... I miss so many people... but Charlie was the first after

the Change that we said goodbye to.
I miss him. I miss him a lot.

TWELVE

"We've had it," Molly said, a few hours later. We were on the outskirts of Leeds on a bridge overlooking the main motorway out of the city. The road we needed to get on to reach home. Only it was beginning to dawn on us that it wasn't going to be an easy drive.

"Just once, we should catch a break," Cara cursed, close to tears. "I mean, it's not that much to ask, is it?"

Apparently it was. So far we'd been lucky with traffic, but there and then our luck seemed to run out. The road ahead was one mass pile-up. The drive into the city had been tricky, manoeuvring around crashed and abandoned cars, but it was at least passable. One look at the motorway below told us that way was closed. I'd never seen a pile-up before, but the motorway was a graveyard to dead cars and their drivers. Many of which were still managing to move and crawl over and around the wreckage of the vehicles.

"There must've been a crash when the Change happened," Pete said.

Kim's hand tightened around mine slightly.

The bypass above the road had been relatively clear. We'd stopped a couple of zombies before deciding it was safe enough to check out our route. Cars were strewn across the lanes, some piled on top of each other, some almost fused together and little more than a burnt-out mess of metal. It was as though a child had got bored playing with his cars and started to hurl them around in a tantrum. Worse still were the zombies. A lot looked like they'd been crash victims after the Change and wandered aimlessly through the ruined scraps of car, limbs missing and horrific wounds covering their battered and torn corpses.

Molly cursed under her breath.

"It's going to be a long journey," she sighed, sounding more defiant than beaten. "And dangerous. We'll have to take side roads and force our way through. Just hope the coach is up for it. She's already starting to look a little battered. What are you two smiling at?" she asked, looking at Kim and me.

"You," I said. "You're pretty cool, you know that? The rest of us are still trying to take this in, but you're already planning a way around it."

"We've come this far," Molly said, blushing at the compliment. "We've lost friends and if we don't make it, their deaths… well, I'm not going to let a few stiffs stop us now. What worries me is what happens when we get somewhere the coach can't get around or through. When there's nowhere else to go."

"There's always another way," I said, as we started back to the transport. "Always."

So we drove. Around and sometimes through the dead. The motorway was impassable. Most cars were abandoned, some locked, their living dead occupants still inside, waiting for the traffic jam to subside. They were going to have a long wait. Others had crashed and burned, the metal starting to bend and fuse. It was hard to tell where one car ended and another began. Looking around, it seemed to me that the world would never stop burning. So we used side roads and bypasses, occasionally braving a section of motorway and zooming down the hard shoulder, ignoring the hungry cries of the dead as they crawled from the wreckage of the world around them to try and follow us. We ignored bollards and one way signs and cones. A grim Doug and Billy were in the Jag, shooting ahead of us like a tracker to see if the way was clear, more often than not returning to let us know it wasn't and we would have to take another, longer route. When the coach slowed down to force its way through tight gaps left by abandoned cars the dead would move in, banging their hands against the sides of the coach. More than once they came close to turning us over. Before the Change, the drive would have taken a couple of hours, max. Now, after eight hours we were less than halfway home and had been forced to turn back yet again to take a different, longer route.

"It's getting hard to see," Molly said, as we approached the outskirts of a small town. "We'll need to stop soon."

Rain had started to pour down, making our path even more treacherous as darkness started to fall. Molly let Doug know over the walkie-talkies that we needed to find a place to spend the night and the Jag shot off, heading up a nearby hill that had a few houses built off the road.

Kim's hand tightened on mine as she felt me tense. If it was up to me, we'd drive all night to get home, but I also knew that didn't make sense. Without electricity to run them all, the streetlights were dead, and with the motorway filled with wrecks, driving at night was both pointless and dangerous. You'd have to be crazy to do it – or have a death wish. The driving was starting to wear Molly down as well. She looked more tired than the rest of us. She'd grown close to Charlie, but was refusing to let the pain out, instead keeping it bottled up deep inside. The coach wasn't in much of a better state than the rest of us. The cars and wrecks we'd scraped past were quickly starting to take their toll. It was getting to the point where every time we heard a bump or scratch we worried that the coach might be about to give up the ghost. The Jag's headlights shone as Doug returned to us, pulling up at a quiet-looking junction.

"It looks like we've got some luck at last," Doug said over the walkie-talkie. The rain was really starting to hammer down now. "There're two houses up there. Looks like they've just been built. Look safe enough from the outside. Fenced too. Probably so kids couldn't get through. Won't bother us though, and it could help to keep some of the bad guys away."

"Sounds good," Molly said.

What was odd was that she waited for me to nod before continuing.

"Okay, see you up there," she said, starting the engine.

Doug had been right about the houses. They were newly furnished and up for sale and completely empty. Best of all, the steel fence that surrounded them gave us some protection against the dead.

"I'll take first watch," Doug said, as we settled in the living room. A couple of the younger kids started to cry when they saw the inside. It was a show room. A beautiful living room pulled straight from an estate agent's window. Most of all it looked normal. Untouched by the chaos outside.

"It's like the Change never happened," Kim said, tightening her grip on my hand.

"We found some bedding," Rosie said, coming downstairs with a quilt and almost tripping up.

"It's okay," Kegs said, seeing my alarm. "Me and Billy have already swept the house. It's safe as… well, safe as houses."

Rosie laughed at this, making Kegs smile.

Kids were starting to form smaller groups. Lizzie and Billy seemed to be spending a lot of time together and started to blush furiously when Rosie caught them holding hands.

"Candles," Molly said, carefully placing some in the living room and lighting them. "Got them from the supermarket."

"Good call," I smiled, starting to feel tired. "What's for tea?"

"Butties," Pete said. "Lots of butties. And some pies and sausage rolls and stuff. I'll share them out."

"No pizza?" I joked.

"I'd kill for a pizza," Molly said, taking a prepacked sandwich from one of the carrier bags a new kid was passing around. "You okay?" she asked him as he did so.

He nodded and moved on.

"Everyone's helping," Kim said. "You notice that?"

I nodded.

"And they gave you food first," she started to tease. "Because you're the leader."

"I am not the leader," I said. "Really."

Kim smiled.

"I'm not," I repeated. "We're more like a family."

We talked then. Pretty much all those sitting in the room were still awake. For a few precious hours the chaos outside seemed unreal and everything seemed normal. We talked about ourselves and our hopes and what we'd liked best about the world.

"Safe," Cara said. "The best thing about the old world was that it was safe. I mean, we'd see places in the news where people were starving or getting blown up but it'd wash over us. Now we're those people. Only there's no one left to come to our rescue."

There was an awkward silence.

"Maybe we should do a TV show," Kegs said. "You know, like Red Nose Day."

People looked at him as if he was an idiot.

"Hear me out," he continued. "You know how they raise money for charity by wearing red noses? Maybe we could have a Red Nose Day for zombies."

"That's silly," Rosie said, rubbing sleep from her eyes.

"You're right," Kegs said. "Zombies have no money to pay for red noses so maybe we should just paint them red."

A few people tittered at this. A sort of nervous laughter. It didn't feel right to laugh.

"That's an idea," Kim said, joining in. "And maybe we could combine it with a Don't Kill the Living Day."

"How would we publicise it though?" a young kid asked.

"On telly, stupid-head," Rosie stated, bringing real laughter to the room.

"I can see the ads now," Billy said, taking over. "Are you a bloodthirsty zombie? Then remember, this Friday is Don't Kill Anyone Day. For more information, see your local graveyard."

"Now that could catch on," Doug said.

There was a general murmur of agreement to this.

"Maybe we could train them," I suggested.

People looked at me as if I was stupid.

"Well, you know, not to be human again, but to do things. Like clean up and play football."

"Rooney's got the ball," Billy said, mimicking a famous TV sports commentator. "He's gone past one zombie, he's gone past another. Surely nothing can stop him now? Oh no, his leg's fallen off. That's rigor mortis for you."

"Still annoyed about the semi-final?" Doug smiled.

"Yeah," I answered. "Been hoping to go since Christmas."

"Wonder what zombies get for Christmas?" Laura said, her baby brother asleep in her arms.

"Well, if I was a zombie, I'd want some deodorant," Billy suggested, Lizzie laughing and looking at him with something like adoration. Kim elbowed me to point it out and smiled. "I mean are they starting to smell, or are they starting to smell?"

"They're starting to smell!" a few kids shouted out.

"I mean, no wonder we keep running away from them – they stink."

More laughter.

"Soon they won't have to strangle us or anything, they'll just pong us to death. On the plus side we'll be able to smell them a mile off."

"As long as they don't learn to wash," someone said.

"True, if they learn to wash we've had it," Billy said. "Or learn kung fu. Ninja zombies would be really bad."

"I hate ninja zombies," Kim said. "Boo hiss to ninja zombies."

Everyone in the room joined in a massive boo-hiss... and so it went. Well into the night. We joked and we laughed and we sometimes cried and we made fun of the zombies and the terror and the fear. By the end of it we all felt even closer.

"Gabs would have enjoyed this," I whispered to Kim.

"There'll be other nights like it," she replied. "And Molly said you should reach home tomorrow."

"What about you?" I asked. "Don't you want to go home?"

Kim shook her head. "Nothing there for me. We'd just moved, so I had no friends and my folks are... were in France. It's just me and Lizzie now."

"You'll like Gabs," I said, holding Kim close and trying my best to comfort her.

"I'm glad we came back for you," she said, starting to drift off into sleep.

"Me too," I whispered. "Me too."

THIRTEEN

"Alex, wake up. They're here."

A voice was yelling at me. Kids were shouting. Reality started to come back.

So much for the peace of the night before.

"The zombies, they've broke through the fence. We have to go!" Kim was shouting. "We have to go right now!"

I rushed to the door of the house. The fence had just fallen and the dead were starting to stagger over it towards us. Fifty or sixty yards away at best.

"Brought this," Rosie said, handing me my club. "Chris is getting everyone up. Which is funny because he's not very good in the mornings…" Her voice trailed off as she saw the mass of dead making their slow and inevitable way towards us.

"You're a life-saver," I said, taking the club from her as Molly and Doug rushed past me.

"We've got to get the coach and Jag before they reach them," Molly said.

"You sort the transport, I'll make sure everyone's ready," Kegs said from behind me, wrapping a protective arm around the scared Rosie and leading her back into the house. "Come on, you'll need to help me."

"We're going to have to ditch the car," I said, as we neared the coach.

"But I love that car," Doug said, before noticing that it was already surrounded by zombies. One actually seemed to be trying to look inside, as though he was thinking of buying it.

"I'll get you another one," I said, as we reached the coach – moments before the dead. The zombies started to move around the coach. A tidal wave of dead flesh.

"Now would be a good time to open the door," I urged, batting a zombie's grasping arm to one side.

"I'm trying, I'm… got it!" Molly shouted, as the door opened. She leapt on and switched the engine on, the coach growling into life – and getting the attention of more zombies.

Doug and me looked at each other, swinging our weapons in front of us, trying to hold the zombies at bay.

"After you," I said.

"No, after you," Doug shouted.

"Not a time to argue about politeness," I replied. "Get on the coach, I'll cover you."

"You'll trip up," he replied. "Get on the coach. I'm bigger and more used to fighting than you."

"Will one of you just get on the coach?" Molly yelled, adding a few swear words for good measure.

Not wanting to waste more time, I turned and leapt on board, only for something to grab my left ankle and trip me up. I went crashing forward, cursing as my elbows smacked against the top step. Cursing even louder when I realised a dead hand had now grabbed my leg and was trying to pull me off the coach. Doug was behind me and brought his bat down on the dead arm, making the hands spasm open and allowing me to scramble free. An instant later I returned the favour, pushing my club forward to hold back a fat woman's hungry arms as she tried to give Doug a deadly hug. As soon as she fell back, the coach doors closed.

"Knew you'd trip up," he laughed.

"We've got a problem," Molly said, revving the coach's engine. "There are so many zombies, it's hard to drive. Let alone turn. You better hold on, I think this is going to get a little messy."

"Put your foot down, we've got to get to the house before them – or we won't be able to get everyone on board."

The coach sputtered forward and we got to the house with seconds to spare, skidding to a halt in front of the door, the zombie horde less than a dozen yards away. Our gang almost flew on board. Laura and the baby came on first, the stretcher with Matt second. The younger kids came on next, Rosie and Chris helping them. By the time the last of our friends got aboard, the zombies were all around the coach again, their movement rocking it to the side, threatening to turn us over.

"Drive!" I yelled, as the door snapped shut. A young-looking zombie banged on the door, confused and angry – as though he'd just missed the bus.

"Really?" Molly answered. "I was going to wait for a while, see if some of the zombies wanted a lift!"

She put her foot down this time, the coach crashing through the sea of dead and, more than once, threatening to spin out of control off the path. For one terrible moment it looked like we were going to actually flip over, both wheels on the left leaving the ground. They landed again with a thud and something started to scrape under the coach. A problem for later. For once we got lucky. We didn't crash. We kept going and pulled free of the mass of dead. We drove straight through the gates, the glass on the windscreen splintering as a stray bit of metal struck it – and then we were free and back on the open road.

"Right," Molly said. "Next stop – your house." She turned to look at me. "Which way was it again?"

FOURTEEN

"We're not going to make it."

"We're going to make it."

"We're not going to make it," Billy mumbled by my side.

Five hours of constant driving, stopping for nothing, had taken us to the outskirts of St Helens. So close to home we could almost taste it. Although the dark fumes coming from the engine at the back of the coach stopped us tasting anything but acrid smoke.

Billy suggested we pull over and, normally, when in a smoking coach that had been leaking oil for ten miles, that would have been an excellent idea. There was one flaw in the plan though, as Molly had pointed out.

"We are surrounded by bloody zombies," she cursed, putting her foot down on the accelerator.

It was a fair point. The dead were crawling and walking out of the houses lining the main road into the town centre and starting to stagger after us.

"Nice to have a welcoming committee," Doug said.

"Hey," Kegs said, looking out of the window. "That's my Uncle Bertie."

A few kids looked at him and said they were sorry.

"It's okay," Kegs said. "I never liked him."

"We're not stopping for nothing," Molly said, crashing through an abandoned Mini.

"Anything," I corrected. "We're not stopping for anything."

"Exactly. Now hold on, we may experience some turbulence."

"We're not going to make it," Billy said again, almost trembling with fear.

"Of course we're going to make it," Lizzie said, slapping him over the head. "And what did I say?"

"Don't be so negative."

"Exactly. Now what's going to happen?"

"We're all going to die," Billy screamed, adding, "Bus!"

Molly swerved at the last second, taking us around the overturned bus with a terrifying skid.

"Is it just me or is the smoke getting thicker?" I asked.

"The back seat's on fire!" a young kid said. "The back seat's on fire!"

"I thought I said no smoking!" Molly yelled, and then added a mildly scary and hysterical laugh. "That'll probably be the engine. You know, Billy might just have a point this time."

"We'll make it," I said. "We're too close not to."

We were lucky. Not many people had been out and about on Good Friday in St Helens, so the roads were relatively clear. By eight on a Friday a lot of people would have gone home from work and been getting ready to go out.

"You're driving on the wrong side!" I shouted, without thinking, trying to ignore the panicked shouts from the back of the coach as some people tried to put out the fire.

"So give me a ticket. I'm also driving without a licence and

I'm under age and the whole world is full of zombies, so driving down the wrong side of the road is the last thing to worry about. Left or right?"

"What?"

"Left or right? I'm not from around here, am I? So I don't know where the TA Centre is."

At least that's almost what she said. In reality she added a few swear words. Okay, so she added a lot more swear words, but you get the idea.

"Left," I said. "It's at the bottom of Prescot Road. Just on the other side of the town centre."

"You sure it'll be safe?" she asked, as we arrived at the east side of town, which I always thought of as the back end of St Helens. It was the grimmest part, a mess of intersecting bypasses with a few grey retail parks thrown in the middle of it all. It was devoid of life at the best of times.

A fire was still burning from what used to be a petrol station and, by the look of things, the flames had spread into the surrounding shops and buildings of the town centre.

As the coach pushed its way through the centre, my heart sank. The town was completely destroyed. The old bingo hall where my gran used to go was a smouldering ruin, the nearby bus shelter almost empty – just a few zombies hanging around the bus stops. A double-decker had crashed into the newsagent and another had fallen onto its side.

"Probably the bus to Liverpool," I mumbled.

"You okay?" Kim asked.

"It's dead," I said. "The whole town. Everyone I know. My folks, my uncles and aunties… everyone."

"They might not be," Kim said, as we reached the end of the small main street of burnt-out shops.

Money was blowing out of a bank. A car was stuck in the main doors and I got the feeling looters had run amok in the place. Not much use for money now though.

One of the town's main pubs looked like a bomb had hit it. It was sad, I had liked the place. Everyone in my sixth form did – it was the only place in town that would serve you under age.

The town's only book shop had been smashed up and looted too. There was a zombie standing outside, and I'm not sure but I think it was the woman who used to own it. I couldn't be certain though. She was always nice to me. Or had been.

Then we were through and so close to home. Less than ten minutes' walk from my house. Just up the hill from the TA Centre we were heading to.

"The road forks here," I said. "You need to take the right one and the TA Centre's at the bottom of the hill. Gate's around the side. If you go up a bit, it's the little road to the right."

We were closer now. Seconds away.

"I'm guessing that's not a welcoming committee," Kegs said, moving to my side.

"Zombies," Molly said. "Lots of them too. Could be a problem."

On cue the coach seemed to cough. A death rattle as it spluttered to a stop.

"No, not now. Not when we're so close," Molly said, almost crying as she turned the key in the ignition and stroked the dashboard with her left hand. "Come on, just give me a little bit more. Please. Just for me."

The engine kicked into life.

"Thank you," Molly said.

"There's someone in the window," Kegs said, as the coach jerked to life.

Kids were moving from the back of the coach now.

"We could be okay – if this rust-bucket can get us to the gate."

"It's not a rust-bucket," Molly said. "It's the greatest coach in the history of the world. If this coach was a boy, I'd marry it."

She put her foot down on the pedal, the brakes screaming.

"I think the coach is going to explode," Kegs said.

"No, it's not," Molly said. "At least it's not until we're safe."

"I think you might be a bit mad," I whispered.

"Me too," Molly grinned, taking her foot off the brakes. "And Billy's right. We're not going to make it. I know this coach. Much more of this and it's dead. There's no way it can get up the hill through all those zombies. Worse still, it could flip and then we'd be in real trouble."

"Right, 'cause like this isn't real trouble," I said.

We looked at each other and burst out laughing. I'm still amazed how some of us laugh when death is close and others go to pieces.

"Get us as close to the doors as you can. We'll have to make it on foot."

"Okey-dokey," Molly said, slamming her foot on the brakes and turning the coach into a tailspin, spinning it around so the doors were close to the entrance of the building. "Not much of a plan," she grinned. "Though it's definitely better than my idea."

"And that is?"

"Death in a blazing fireball, taking as many of these things with us as we can."

"Let's call that Plan B," I smiled, holding on as the coach skidded to a halt, kids screaming with fright behind us, a few falling into the gangway.

The wooden doors were about eight yards away from us – and between us and them at least twenty zombies – some in a pretty bad state but all more than able to tear us apart.

"Er, guys, the fire's starting to spread," Kegs said. "I think the coach is about to die."

A couple of kids were lifting a fragile-looking Matt down the aisle, his leg dragging behind him.

"I think you might be right," Molly said.

"Kegs, get ready. We're going to clear a path to the doors."

"You mean the locked doors with no way through?" he said.

"That's right," I said.

"Why aren't they opening the doors?" Kim asked. "They must have seen us."

"Okay," Kegs shouted. "Doug, Billy, grab the bats. We need to clear a path for the others."

"You know we don't stand a chance?" Kim whispered to us, as Molly prepared to open the coach's door.

"We've got to try," I answered, grabbing her hand for what could have been one last time. "Molly, open the door."

There was a creak as the doors whirred open one last time. Dead arms lashed out straight away. A bald fat thing tried to crawl up the steps, only to be met by Kegs' Doc Marten boots.

"He shoots, he scores," Kegs laughed, bringing his bat down on another.

The odds were against us. We couldn't even get off the coach. The burning, soon-to-explode coach!

We were dead.

"Knew we weren't going to make it," Billy said from behind me, only to be slapped on the back of the head again by Lizzie.

"Sorry," he mumbled.

Shots rang out from above and the zombies directly in front of us collapsed to the ground. Cadets could be seen at the windows of the TA Centre, using guns to clear our path to the doors. At first we didn't know what had happened, but the doors in front of us opened and eight soldiers appeared, dressed in what looked like riot gear and carrying police batons, their faces covered by riot masks. They formed two lines either side of the coach's doors, holding back the dead.

"Well, what are you waiting for?" one of them yelled. "An invite!?"

We didn't need to be told twice.

"Get Laura and Matt in first," I shouted. "Then the kids."

Within seconds, we were off the coach and running towards the welcoming doors of the TA Centre – apart from Molly, who seemed to be messing around by the driver's seat. The flames at the rear of the coach were now snaking down the seats.

"Molly, come on. I know you like the coach but we've got to go now!"

"Just making sure she goes out in style!" Molly yelled, starting the engine and slapping a heavy bag on the accelerator. Taking her foot from the brakes, she leapt off the coach as it started its last journey down the hill into the mass of dead trying to reach us.

We ran to the doors, the soldiers backing in behind us with military precision. As they slammed the doors closed, we rushed to a window in the entrance hall, watching as the now blazing coach moved slowly through the sea of dead, flames rushing out of the windows and billowing in the wind. Something about it reminded me of a swan gliding across a lake.

We were amazed how far it got before grinding to a halt.

"She's making sure we're safe," Molly sniffed, tears flooding down her cheeks. "When she goes she wants to make sure it's far enough away from us so we don't get caught in the blast."

"You're mad," Kegs said, but something in the tone of his voice made me think he was a little in awe of the coach.

"Do not go gentle into that good night, rage, rage against the dying of the light," Molly whispered.

The coach exploded.

All of us ducked for cover, worried the glass of the windows might smash in the blast. All apart from Molly, who just stood there, staring at the last moments of her coach.

"Now that is the way to go," she said, a melancholy smile crossing her face before she turned to us. "See, told you we'd make it."

"Ahem," one of the rescuers coughed.

I turned just in time to see him remove his helmet.

"Fancy meeting you lot here," Glover grinned.

FIFTEEN

No one moved.

We were crammed into the entrance hall of the TA Centre, a line of our 'saviours' in front of us – all with guns. Glover was at the front, his gun pointing straight at me.

And my first thought?

Gabs.

I'd told her to come to the TA Centre. That she'd be safe there.

Guess I'd been wrong.

"Ha, if you could see your face!" Glover laughed.

"Doug was right. We should've killed them," Kegs whispered by my side.

Boom.

Glover shot the glass out of the window behind us.

"Did I give you permission to talk?" he snapped, "No. I didn't. Now drop those stupid weapons."

None of us did. Two more of his crew appeared on a staircase to our left. Machine guns in their hands.

"Oh come on. You've got bats. We've got guns. We win," Glover said. "Or have you already forgotten what happened to that stupid Chinese kid?"

"Easy," I whispered, aware that Doug was moving forward, tense and filled with hatred. "Do as he says. At least for now."

The sound of the bats and clubs dropping echoed through the corridor.

"Boy, this is fun. The gang's all here. You must be so pleased with yourselves. Well, not now obviously, but a few seconds ago when you thought you were all home safe."

"Where's my brother?" Matt's tired and worried voice called out from the back.

I glanced back to see Matt leaning against a wall, sweat pouring down his face. It looked like it was taking his last reserves of energy to stand. Billy was nearby, trying to help him.

"Who?" Glover asked.

"His brother," Rosie said suddenly. "His name's Johnny and he should be here. He should be the one in charge."

"Isn't she the little firecracker?" Glover said, sinking to one knee to look into her eyes. "You're the brat who hid on the coach, ain't you? You're the one who made me and my sister fall out."

"You did that yourself by being so mean," Rosie said.

For a second I thought Glover was going to hit her. Instead he just got to his feet and started laughing again. There was nothing remotely sane about the sound of his laughter.

"Aww, ain't she cute?" Glover said. "If she talks again, I'm gonna shoot her."

To her credit, Rosie didn't cry but she did look truly terrified. Kegs stepped forward and placed a protective arm around her.

"I remember you," Glover said, sounding more like an animal than a human being. "And you," he added, pointing at Doug. "But most of all, I remember you," he said, staring at me with pure hatred. "You're the kid who blindsided me."

I didn't know what to say but then, glancing around his gang, realised one face in particular was missing.

"Where's your sister?" I asked.

"Dead," he said. "And you should know that. You killed her."

He fell silent for a moment and looked at the gun in his hand. I had the strangest feeling he was trying to work out whether to kill me or not.

"Now, get in the gym at the end of the hall. We've been expecting you."

"Let's go," I said, starting to move forward myself, watching Glover's gang follow our every move.

And my friends, it has to be said, were holding their nerve pretty well. No one was crying or whimpering. They were silent and shocked, but also waiting.

At least until we saw the state of those in the gym.

"The poor kids," I heard Kim whisper to herself, covering her mouth in shock.

The first thing I noticed was the despair. I'm not sure if that's good English but it's the only way I can describe the shell-shocked and broken kids huddled inside. Before, it had been a five-a-side pitch. Now it was a refugee camp (make that prison) for the truly desperate and broken. About fifty kids were there. All hungry and tired. Turned out they hadn't eaten for more than a day and had been left there, locked in, since the takeover. The stink was appalling. We once did the Black Hole of Calcutta in History. Look it up if you've never heard of it, and then picture it full of kids who'd already gone through hell and you might start to get an idea of what it was like.

"Where's all the older kids?" I asked. "The Cadets? What have you done with them?"

"Sent them for a little walk with their boss – that'll be Johnny," Glover laughed. "They didn't seem to like my plans for the place."

People shuffled out of the way but none looked Glover in the eye.

I moved forward as well, only to be stopped by Glover.

"No you don't," Glover said, as I tried to follow my friends. "Me and you, we need to have a little talk."

I glanced at his gun. One of his friends pointed another at my head.

"I know what you're thinking," Glover cackled. "You're thinking, I bet I could take him. But you can't. You got lucky last time. Now come on, before I lose my patience."

Glover started walking out of the gym and his lackey pushed me after him.

"Step this way, into my office," he laughed.

"You're not taking him anywhere," Kegs said.

Glover was quick, too quick for Kegs. He smacked the side of Kegs' head with the butt of his gun. Kegs dropped to one knee and was about to attack when we heard guns and rifles click around us. Rosie screamed, her brother holding her back. It was all threatening to kick off, and with the guns involved there was no way it would end well for us. I didn't want to see any more friends hurt.

I couldn't see any more friends hurt.

The kids around us were still silent, but some were looking at my friends with a mixture of fear and hope.

"It's okay," I said, trying to calm things down. "We're just going to have a little chat. I'll be fine."

Glover laughed out loud at this, which really didn't help the situation, as he led me out of the hall and up the stairs to a room on the first floor.

"Good to see you again," he smirked as we entered the room. "We have so much catching up to do. You know, the pressures of leadership, how to kill zombies and what to do with sisters. Especially dead sisters."

"Nice place, innit?" Glover grinned, snapping my worried mind back to the room.

It used to be the caretaker's flat, but Glover had converted it into his own base. There was the biggest TV I'd ever seen pushed against one wall with all the latest consoles next to it. The place was filled with expensive electronic equipment and bags of jewellery and cash. Scattered against the wall was a pile of knives and bats and other weapons – including a samurai sword. As Glover talked, a couple of his crew added our own weapons to the pile. The baseball bats and golf clubs looked out of place amongst their deadlier cousins.

"Turns out this town's got a few good shops," Glover grinned, sitting behind a desk and putting his feet on it, hands behind his head, like some mad general from an old war movie.

"Oh, don't look so worried," he said. "I've not killed your precious little sister. I couldn't do that."

Relief washed over me.

"Mainly because I've not had the chance to look for her yet. What with getting supplies and taking this place over. I was hoping she'd be here so I could have her dead body waiting for you. As a sort of welcome-home present, you know? That would've been a right laugh. But she wasn't here so now you're going to help me to find her."

I didn't say anything.

"You see, the last time we met was kind of a low point for me. Truth to tell, I'd taken a few things I shouldn't and wasn't at my best. Then you fed my mates to the zombies and left me and my sister to die. That sort of thing can really make you feel miserable, you know?"

"You're mad," I whispered.

"Nah," Glover said, shaking his head. "I was at first. When you lot legged it and left me and my sister to die. Then I was all screams and 'I'm gonna kill ya' and stuff but now I'm fine with it. I reminded myself of something my gran used to say. An eye for an eye. Or was it a pie for a pie? No, I'm pretty sure it was an eye for an eye. Which means you killed my sister so now I'm going to kill yours. Easy-peasy lemon squeezy. If you think about it, like."

"We didn't kill anyone," I said.

"You set zombies on my crew!" he yelled, losing his temper for the first time and smashing his fist onto the desk. "I had to force them to fight. Hell, I even had to shoot a couple of them so the others wouldn't leg it. And my sister. My poor little sister – you left her to die."

"That's not true," I said, sensing my own death was close. "We asked her to come with us but she chose not to. She chose to stay with you. And there was still time to get out…"

"Liar!" Glover yelled, tears streaming down his face. "Liar, liar, pants on fire! She stayed because you made her and when the zombies came in she stayed because she knew I was the only one who could sort you lot out. She knew I had to get away."

A thought hit me then. A thought so horrific it hardly seemed believable. But something I knew instinctively to be true.

"You left her," I whispered. "You left your own sister to die and you ran. You ran like a scared little kid."

"It didn't happen like that," he cried out, jumping from behind the desk to face me. "It was your fault. It was all your fault."

The gun was there again. I closed my eyes and waited for the trigger to be pressed.

Nothing happened. When I opened them again, Glover was back to normal. Or at least what passed for normal in his case.

"Cigarette?" he said, offering me one as if we were old friends.

"Only idiots smoke," I said.

"Yeah, well, that's me. A right old idiot. I went easy on you lot last time. I should have killed you all, but I thought, no. Fair's fair. Give them a fighting chance. And look where it got me."

Glover fell silent for a minute.

"So anyway, I managed to get out of the shop, obviously 'cause I'm here now, and it didn't take me that long to track a few of the crew down and we thought, what now, and then I remembered what Stacy had told me about you lot heading to the TA Centre and it being safe and stuff and then I thought how nothing was safe for me and mine and how that didn't really seem very fair so I thought, right, that needs to be sorted, so we shot up here nonstop, and then we got here and your pal Johnny, I tell you, he was such a nice guy. So trusting and everything. So we beat him up and took over. Job done. Did you know there's an armoury? How cool is that? I mean they had some kid guarding it, but he was a bit soft and then some of the older kids seemed to be upset about it all but by then we had the guns so we had to ask them to leave and then we just waited for you guys to show up. Got to admit, I was starting to get worried you'd been killed or something. I mean it's dangerous out there, you got to be real careful these days. But anyway, you made it, which is great because if you hadn't my whole plan would have been a complete waste of time and then when you did turn up I thought should I let the zombies eat you and then I thought, no, where's the fun in that? And then I had the brainwave. I'd help you find your sister and then kill her while you watch. Revenge sorted."

I was too dumbstruck by the sheer craziness of what I'd just heard to even think about his words.

"Oh, don't look so miserable," he said, prodding me with the gun in what I think was a bizarre effort to cheer me up. "Look on the bright side – I'm going to kill you straight after so you'll be together again. And you won't grow old and become zombies. So, in a way, I'll be doing you both a big favour."

"If you think I'm going to help you to find my sister you're even crazier than I thought."

"Hmm, good point," Glover said, looking thoughtful for a moment. "Okay, how about this? I'll give you a choice. We find your sister or I kill your friends. All of them – even the little ones."

"What?"

"You heard me," Glover said. "Simple choice. Your sister for your friends. Deal or no deal?"

SIXTEEN

"Do I look stupid?" Glover asked, as the car pulled up outside a house not far from mine.

I decided not to answer the question.

There were three of us in a military jeep. I was in the back with Glover. A tall, skinny kid called Mack was driving.

"I got your address from one of the kids at the TA, didn't I?" Glover laughed. "That's your house over there. Nice try though. I'll give you that. Was that the plan? Lead me into a strange house and then try to kill me?"

Taking them to the wrong house was the only thing I could think of on the short trip home. After agreeing to take him to my house – mainly to buy time – he'd led me straight out of the TA Centre to the parade ground and the garages that were at the back. A few jeeps and trucks were parked there.

"Mack here can drive," Glover had said. "Roads are pretty clear out back. Since you arrived, all the zombies have been massing at the front. Hoping to have a second chance at you and yours I guess."

The streets were pretty empty, even though it was just past lunchtime. Not that there was anyone left to have lunch. I did spot a couple of neighbours shuffling around. One, Mr Clark, who lived in a bungalow at the bottom of my road, was standing in his garden looking down at his lawnmower as though it was an old friend whose name he couldn't remember.

"Look at that nutter!" Glover laughed, shooting him as the car drove by.

"Why did you do that?" I yelled, as his body crumpled to the ground.

"It was a laugh, wasn't it? And anyway, don't wet your pants. He's not really dead. Look."

"But there could be a cure," I said, glancing back to see the zombified Mr Clark stagger back to his feet, his dead eyes staring at the hole in his side as though it was a nasty stain. "We should only hurt them if it's in self-defence. One day they might work out what caused this and find a way of turning them back."

"Oh God, I hope not," Glover said. "That would be so boring. So which house is yours?"

And that was when I tried pointing to the wrong one and he laughed. A few seconds later, he was pushing me towards my own.

The neighbour came out to pay her respects. Mrs Greenham was a nice old lady, well into her retirement. Death had not been kind to her. It looked like she'd fallen downstairs, her body all twisted and broken, old bones sticking through old flesh. She wasn't a danger to us, the small fence dividing our houses proving way too much for her mangled form.

For once, Glover looked thoughtful and quiet.

"Wonder what it's like?" he asked.

I had the feeling it was a rhetorical question.

For my part I wasn't really listening. The full impact of my surroundings were starting to hit.

I was home.

We were walking up the small drive to the house. Slightly to our left was the old garage, Dad's car parked outside. To the right, the front door. I half expected it to open and Rebel, our Alsatian, to come bounding out to greet me. She was a big fan of greeting family members. Part of me even expected my parents to be there, telling me it was okay. That everything was going to be okay from now on.

It seemed a lifetime ago I'd left. I remember my mum waving goodbye, making me feel embarrassed. Didn't realise it was the last time I'd see her.

My eyes started to grow misty.

"Oh don't get all girly on me," Glover said, patting me on my back as though he was an old friend. "You'll be dead soon, so none of this'll matter. Course I will too, but at least I'll still be walking."

"What do you mean?" I asked.

"You really are dumb, aren't you?" Glover said. "It's my birthday, ain't it? My eighteenth birthday. Any moment now I'm going to die and become one of them. Well, not one of them exactly. I reckon I'm going to be okay. Better than ever in fact."

A thought crept into my mind.

"So what time were you born?" I asked, pretending to look for the keys.

"That's for me to know and for you to find out," Glover grinned. "Don't worry though. Got plenty of time to get me a present – and to find your sister. Now get the door open. I want to get this show on the road."

"I've no keys," I lied, playing for time. "They're in my rucksack back in the Retreat."

"Time-wasting, hey?" Glover laughed. "Doesn't matter. It's only a door – and who needs doors these days?"

Glover leaned over the rockery and pulled up one of the larger stones, hurling it at the front window.

"Wow, did you see that smash?" he laughed as it shattered. "That was so cool. After you…"

I carefully climbed in through the window, removing a few dangerous shards of broken glass as I did so, half expecting to see Dad burst into the front room yelling about the noise. My home wasn't the biggest in the town, but it wasn't the smallest. It had three bedrooms upstairs and two rooms and a kitchen downstairs. The front room was only used when visitors turned up – or me and Dad wanted to watch something on the other TV when a soap opera was on.

"It's home," I whispered, momentarily forgetting everything around me.

There was a wedding photo on the wall. My folks were only a little older than me when they got married. They looked so happy. The old record player in the corner was a present from my auntie, along with a bunch of old records she'd left behind when she'd got married and moved out. There were some great old punk singles in there way older than me. Some worth a mint. Not that I'd ever have sold them. They were way too cool to sell.

Memories came rushing back without warning. I remembered being ill as a child, during one of the rare occasions we decided to use the front room as a living room. I was curled up on the couch, a blanket over me. Drifting in and out of sleep with the warm sound of my parents nearby. Don't think I'd ever felt as safe as I did back then. A new thought entered my head. One I'd been trying my best to ignore for days.

What if my folks were here – and they'd changed? What was I going to do if I had to face my own zombified parents?

"Come on, let's get a move on," Glover said, prodding me forward again. "Mack, check upstairs."

I allowed myself the faintest of smiles as I felt the breeze coming through from the kitchen where the door to the back garden was. If it was open the chances were Gabs had made it out of the house.

Or something had made it in.

We left the front room and I jumped as I saw something move to my left.

It was my own reflection, looking back at me from the full-length mirror hanging in the hall.

"Yeah, you do look pretty scary," Glover mocked, pausing to wink at his own reflection.

The door to the living room at the back of the house was closed.

"Open it," Glover said.

I had my hand on the door and was frozen. More memories were rushing back. Lying on the floor doing my homework. Helping my dad lay the new carpet a couple of years before. The excitement of getting a new and much better TV. All these images and more flooded over me as I slowly pushed the door open.

"Well, it's not looking good for sis, is it?" Glover laughed.

The living room itself was just how I'd left it. The TV in the corner dominating the room. The black leather couch against the far wall (my favourite place to sprawl while reading). On the dining table was the homework I'd accidentally left behind when going away and a half finished cup of tea (that just had to be my dad's. He could drink tea for England. At least that's what my mum used to say). There was a painting a friend of my mum's had done hanging on the wall over the fireplace showing boats at sea. On the window ledge were a few books – including an old paperback I'd been reading.

"No sign of anyone upstairs," Mack said, entering the living room and then adding a few swear words when he looked out of the large back window into the garden beyond.

Twenty to thirty zombies were on the lawn. At the rear of the garden, just beyond the back of the garage, a truck had crashed into the side wall and come to rest in my dad's greenhouse. The windscreen was smashed to pieces and the front of the truck itself pretty mangled. There was a nursing home next to my parents' house and the truck had crashed in from there, most of the dead residents following it. Many were still in dressing gowns and pyjamas as they staggered about.

Dad's not going to like what've they've done to his lawn, I thought, noticing how muddy it was under their dead feet.

They were just standing there, all of them, staring at the garage. One of them was carrying something in his hand.

A girl's red jacket.

The moment I saw it, the zombie – an old man I recognised as the owner of the house at the back of ours – turned and looked at me, his dead eyes staring straight into my own.

"This ain't going according to plan at all," Glover complained.

For a second I thought he was going to give up, but then he saw the jacket as well.

"Well, look at that," he grinned. "If my eyes don't deceive me, that's just the sort of coat a little kid might really like and might lose when rushing to her hiding place in… oh, I don't know, the garage maybe?"

I thought about making a run for it, but Glover must have read my mind and raised his gun.

"Don't even think about it," he smiled.

Mack was still staring out at the garden and the dead there. As they saw us move, they turned and started to shamble towards the window. Within a few seconds the first, a little old man whose black toupee was somehow still on his head, was clawing at the glass, trying to get to us. Another joined him. A male nurse by the look of it, with a bald head and a fresh nasty-looking scar down the left side of his face.

"That's not going to last long," Mack said, looking at the window and sounding scared.

"Let's get out there then," Glover said, directing me to the door.

I moved, but Mack obviously thought it was a bad idea.

"Maybe we should just forget about the kid," he said. "Not worth getting killed over, is it?"

"Don't tell me you're going soft," Glover said.

"No," Mack answered. "Just don't want to be torn apart by zombies, that's all."

It seemed to me he was trying to work out who was the scariest – the dead or Glover.

Unfortunately for me, Glover won.

"Come on," Mack said, pushing me out of the door a little too viciously. Think he was trying to prove something to Glover. "Let's get this over with."

"That's more like it," Glover grinned.

The pounding on the glass was louder now as a couple more dead had joined in. Mack pushed me into the kitchen and I found myself facing Mr Gregly, a builder from down the road. A dead builder from down the road.

He growled angrily and moved towards me.

"Down, Fido," Glover said, smacking the butt of his rifle into the zombie's face, then a few times more to be sure he wasn't going to be a problem.

I seized my chance and rushed out into the garden.

"Hey, wait up!" Glover laughed. "Aren't you going to thank me for saving your life?"

I paused on the small patio outside the kitchen. Luckily for me, most of the dead were following their friends to the living-room window and had thinned out from the lawn. It gave me the chance to rush the short distance across the garden to the old garage, skipping out of the way of a couple of pairs of dead outstretched arms as I did so. By the time I got to the small door at the side of the garage, I could see Mack and Glover on the patio. Glover was laughing, like he had all the time in the world.

"Gabs!" I yelled. "We've got to get out of here. It's not safe!"

I burst into the garage and, for a second, thought I could see my sister standing in the shadows.

But it wasn't her, just a few bags of sand my dad had piled up for a future job. The only light was through the small square window in the wall. A window that I don't think had been cleaned for as long as I'd been alive – if not longer. On a shelf near the side was a torch, almost hidden among a pile of rusted tools and boxes of nails and screws.

I heard shouting behind me and saw Mack getting attacked by a couple of zombies, while Glover stood nearby laughing – the zombies left him alone as he walked towards me.

I flicked the torch on and scanned the garage. Quickly I dragged one of the bags of sand to barricade the door as best I could. It wouldn't buy me much time, but maybe enough. I rushed to the back door and tried to open it, only to curse when I realised it was locked – and the keys would have been somewhere in the house.

I was trapped.

And then I saw it.

Lying on the floor near my feet. A few tins of food, the dog's favourite bone… and a diary.

My sister's diary.

The sound of gunfire came from outside, along with Mack's voice cursing Glover.

I opened the diary at the back page and started to read. The last entry was from the night before.

She was alive. Gabs was alive. For the first time in days a real smile crossed my face.

I can't wait any longer, the entry read. *I've got to go. Alex should've been here by now. I think something bad's happened to him. I tried to go to the TA Centre like he said. I was about to try and get in but then saw some kids getting kicked out. Johnny was with them and looked like he'd been beaten up. So I ran off. I didn't know where to go and by the time I got back here the… the things were in the house. Rebel protected me. They're scared of her – and they should be. She doesn't like them at all. I thought the garage would be a safe place to stay for the night but thinking about it I need somewhere better. Somewhere with food. I'm going to go and try to find Johnny and the others. I'm going to leave this here though. In case Alex is alive. If you're reading this, Alex, don't worry. I'm fine. I hope you are too.*

The door of the garage burst open, the sandbags sliding backwards as Glover entered, laughing insanely.

The sound of gunfire behind him had stopped.

"I was right," he said. "The dead didn't touch me. It's like they know I'm going to be one of them soon. That I'm going to be special."

I pushed myself to my feet, torch in one hand, my sister's diary in the other.

"What's so funny?" Glover asked.

"Gabs is alive," I smiled. Think I was losing it again. It happens. "I win."

"Yeah, but your friends are going to lose," Glover said. "Big time."

He stepped forward and pointed the rifle at me. At first I thought he was going to shoot me. Looking back, I think he did too, but changed his mind and swung the rifle around like a club. It struck the side of my head and sent me crashing to the ground. The torch slid from my hand but I held onto the diary.

Glover loomed above me, as the world started to spin away. My vision was red, the light from the torch creating nightmarish shadows as it rolled along the ground.

"Loser," I said, as Glover brought the butt of his gun down

on me again.
And this time there was nothing.
Nothing at all.

SEVENTEEN

"Wakey, wakey!" a crazed voice was yelling.

I was back at the TA Centre, in the parade ground. Rain was lashing down and I was soaking wet. Lots of kids were gathered around. Some I knew, most I didn't. All looked terrified, some concerned. Pain was pretty much all over my body. My forehead felt odd (turns out it was swollen and bruised), my vision blurred. Judging by the way my friends were looking at me, I was in a bit of a state.

Glover kicked me in the chest. It was hard to breathe and I had the feeling a rib or two was broken. Remember that old cartoon about the Coyote and the Roadrunner? I used to love it when I was a kid (and still do, but don't tell anyone) but always felt a little sorry for the Coyote when the boulders and stuff fell on him. I always thought that it would probably hurt to be the poor old Coyote. Now I knew what it was like and I'd been right. It did hurt. In fact, I don't think there was a bit of my body that wasn't hurting.

"Come on, stop messing around," Glover mocked. "It's only a scratch."

"Gabs," I whispered, pushing myself onto my knees.

The ice-cold rain lashed into my face. It was a life-saver. Like throwing a bucket of water over an unconscious man.

"Found her and killed her," Glover grinned. "Just after I knocked you out."

"Liar, liar, pants on fire," I whispered, only semi-rational at this point.

"You got me," Glover laughed. "Still, at least I have you and your mates to play with."

It was almost dark. The sky was filled with grey storm clouds. I put my hands through my soaking hair and swept it back, using the last of my strength to get to my feet.

It took three attempts. By which point Glover was already doubled up laughing.

"Look at the big hero," he said. "He's going to save everyone. But he's no hero. He beat me up, left my sister to die, sent my crew to their deaths."

"You did all that yourself," I said, spitting out blood.

I had the strangest feeling that I might actually be dying.

"No, I didn't," Glover yelled. "I was trying to help everyone. I had my crew and we were going to get your coach and go somewhere safe. It was sorted. Job done. Then you came along and ruined it all."

I looked around and noticed Kim, Rosie and Kegs were missing from the crowd. Doug was watching with Christopher and the rest of the gang. He looked furious and I got the impression that it was taking all his will power not to launch himself at Glover.

It looked like most of the kids from inside had been dragged out to the yard. Behind them were Mack and the rest of Glover's gang – all pointing their weapons at my friends. Though Mack himself seemed lost in thought. Hardly surprising as his left arm was bandaged badly and he had a nasty gash on his leg. The dead themselves were no longer massing at the front. All the movement and noise from the back had attracted them to the parade ground. There seemed to be a hundred, if not more, gathering on the other side of the steel fence.

Waiting.

It was as if they knew their chance was coming.

That death was close.

"If you're wondering where your friends are, a few of them legged it. First chance they got. That's loyalty for you."

Doug winked as Glover spoke and I smiled and started laughing.

"What's so funny?" Glover asked.

"My friends wouldn't leave me," I said. "You've lost. You just don't know it yet."

"I've lost?" Glover shouted. "I've lost? And they call me crazy. You're the one who's lost, mate. You're the one who's about to die."

"So shut up and shoot me," I said. "Prove you're better than me."

"Don't need to."

"Course you don't. You don't need to prove anything. You don't need to prove you're a better fighter, a better leader. I'm sure your crew already know that. Mack, for instance. How's the arm?"

Mack looked at me and then looked away, not saying a word.

"Great plan that was," I said to Glover. "Go to mine and get your mate mauled. Real winner."

"He knows it was all part of the plan," Glover said. "He's a good soldier."

"He's not a soldier," I said. "And there is no plan."

"The plan is to get justice for what you did to my crew," Glover shouted, lifting the gun again in my direction. "You have been found guilty of cowardice and murder. The sentence is death."

"Who by?" I asked. "I missed the trial."

"Don't need no trial," Glover snarled. "Everyone knows you're guilty as sin."

"So you're going to execute me. Just like that," I said.

"Yeah, just like that," Glover said, stepping closer and placing the tip of the gun against my forehead.

I'm still not sure where I found the courage from, but I didn't blink or flinch. I just stared at him. I know I was terrified but I guess I was angry too. Angry about everything. My sister, my friends, Charlie and all the dead. I saw Doug still wearing Charlie's bloodstained top around his waist and my anger coldly became something else.

It became a plan.

"So you're going to execute me and then kill all my friends, right? Is your crew okay with that? With committing cold-blooded murder?"

"Changed my mind about that," Glover said. "Since the troublemakers have legged it, your gang's been well behaved. In fact they've said they want me to lead them. Isn't that right, Billy boy?" he said.

"Oh yes, sir. Definitely. You're the best leader ever. So much better than Alex."

Luckily, Glover was so full of himself he failed to notice the sarcasm in Billy's voice.

"See?" Glover said. "I win after all. Your gang are mine and young Billy here's a regular hero. Warned me about your mates legging it. He was the only one saw them jumping over the back fence. Outrageous, isn't it? Still, all's well that ends well. Any last requests?"

"Fight me," I whispered.

What was it Charlie had once said, if you can't beat them, join them? I had a better idea. If you can't beat them, get them to join you.

"I'm not scared of you," Glover said.

"Prove it," I said. "Fight me."

"Fight, fight, fight," Doug started to whisper.

I glanced up at the TA Centre and saw a familiar face looking out of an upstairs window.

I allowed myself a smile.

"Fight, fight, fight." Christopher and Pete joined in.

"Shut up," Glover yelled. "Shut up or I'll kill you all now."

"Fight, fight, fight," Matt started to say, leaning on an old crutch.

"Fight, fight, fight," Glover's crew started to mouth the words.

With a scream of rage, Glover tossed the gun aside and hurled himself at me. A flurry of blows rained down – he was quick and in far better condition than me. One blow hit the side of my temple, still bleeding from his previous attack, and I crumpled to the ground. Glover started bouncing around again, clearly happy with himself.

"Ha, knew it," he laughed. "You're dead on your legs."

I pushed myself to my feet. Still to this day I'm not sure how

I managed it.

"Again," I whispered.

Doug tried to come to my aid but Mack blocked his path – a rifle convincing him to stay put.

"It's okay," I coughed, alarmed at the sight of blood from a split lip. "I got him on the ropes."

Glover rushed me again. I'd love to tell you I found some last vestige of strength hidden away and used it to beat him, but I didn't.

Another punch sent me to the floor.

This really was it, I thought. This really was the end. I just hope I'd bought Kim enough time to rescue everyone.

I'd pushed myself onto one knee and tried to summon the strength for one last round, but it was no use. I could hardly stand. Glover moved in for the kill, kicking me in the face. That's when I lost the tooth. I could see Kim and the others now though, quietly sneaking into the crowd and passing our weapons to everyone while Glover's crew watched the fight.

Spitting the tooth into my hand I somehow managed to raise myself one last time.

"Could you hold this for me?" I asked Mack, giving him the tooth.

He nodded and seemed a little impressed.

"Okay, enough of this," Glover said. "You're finished."

"I don't think so," Kim said.

Everyone turned to see Kim and my friends standing around the yard. Kim was holding a samurai sword in her hand. Next to her, Kegs was holding his favourite club.

"Last chance to give in," I coughed, trying my best not to

pass out.

"You lot can't stop us," Glover said. "We've got guns."

"You have eight guns," Kim said. "We have fifteen golf clubs, six chair legs, five hockey sticks and this rather wonderful samurai sword I found in the caretaker's office. Plus we've stopped zombies. Lots of zombies. You've run away from a few."

"Yeah, and we've got a rounders bat too," Rosie added.

Mack laughed at this. Big mistake. Rosie hit him on the knee. He let out a cry and dropped his gun.

"Seven guns," Doug said, beating Mack to the weapon.

Mack rubbed his knee but smiled. That was the moment I realised we'd won.

"I've had it with this," he said. "Never liked the guy anyway. Just thought I'd have a better chance of survival with him. Think I made a mistake."

"I'll say," Kim said. "You beat up my boyfriend."

"Wasn't him," I said, stepping in between them before Kim could do something she'd regret.

I was also stunned by her words.

"So I'm your boyfriend, am I?" I said, with a smile.

"Bloody better be, after all this," she said.

"No!" Glover screamed, glancing around at his gang who were all now starting to have second thoughts.

"If you want to join us, you're more than welcome," I said. "But do us a favour and lower the weapons. There's been enough violence for one day."

All but one did just that.

"It's not going to end like this," Glover yelled, sounding crazier than ever and rushing towards the gates and waiting zombies. They seemed to sense something was happening and started to growl and push forwards.

"You're not taking my gang from me," Glover screamed. "If I can't win, no one does."

A shot rang out and Glover crumpled to the ground, a few yards from the gate.

"If he'd opened the gates, we wouldn't have had a chance," Mack said, throwing his gun to the ground like it was a venomous snake.

I nodded, and was about to collapse with exhaustion when I heard Doug yell out a warning.

"He's not dead!"

"It's my birthday!" Glover screamed, staggering forward. "And I will not die!"

Another shot rang out from one of his gang. Glover seemed to crumple. None of us moved. Glover crawled towards the gate, pulling out a key and unlocking the gates as he let out a couple of final pitiful gasps.

"I'll be one of you soon, wait and see," he coughed, pushing himself to his feet and raising his arms into the air triumphantly. "I'll be the king of you all. Zombie Number One!"

His final screams were lost as the dead washed over him in one hungry mass.

"Get behind us," Mack yelled, as he moved forward with his six friends and let off a round of gunfire into the mass of dead approaching.

Not that the bullets did any good.

"There's too many," I said, using the last of my strength to help my friends.

I glanced at the TA Centre. The back wasn't as secure as the front.

"We need to get out of here," I said. "The trucks. Get everyone to the trucks."

Kim shouted orders at a few kids and ran towards the garages.

"We'll try to slow them down," Mack said. "It's the least we can do."

I nodded, unable to think of anything to say.

"Alex," Doug yelled. "A couple of kids are still in the Centre. They were too injured to move."

"Kim, get the truck loaded and ready. We're going to get the others."

Kim rushed closer and kissed me.

Despite everything, the rain, the possibility of imminent death from the walking dead, it was a very good kiss.

"You better not die on me," she said.

"No chance," I smiled.

I turned and limped into the building, Doug, Billy, Cara and Kegs alongside me while Kim led the rest of the kids towards the garages.

Only a couple of kids were left in the gym.

"Are the bad people back?" a little girl asked me, looking terrified. Her arm was in a sling and a bandage covered her left leg.

"Yeah," I nodded. "But this time we're badder. In fact, I hear they're scared of us."

"Really?" the kid asked.

"Don't be stupid," another little girl interrupted. "Course they're not scared of us. We're going to get deaded just like everyone else has."

"No, we're not," Rosie said beside me. "We're going to live. Because that's what we do."

"I thought I told you to go with Kim, where it's safe," I said.

"Nowhere's safe, silly," Rosie stated.

"Good point," I conceded. "Okay, let's get out of here."

There was a deathlike growl and, as we left the gym, a couple of zombies came into view.

"No problem, there's only a couple," I said.

Rosie shook her head and pointed as six more of the dead appeared in the corridor, blocking our exit.

Billy and Kegs looked at each other and smiled.

There was something a little crazy and sad about their smiles.

"Geronimo!" the two of them roared, rushing headlong into the dead and forcing them back out of the corridor and into the parade ground beyond.

"Quick!" I yelled. "While they're distracted, get everyone out!"

People didn't need to be asked twice. I went first, using a broken chair leg to beat back a couple of dead while somehow managing to carry a little girl out.

"You're bleeding on my best dress," she said.

"Sorry," I apologised, as a zombie pulled the weapon from my hand. Unsure of what to do, I turned and side-kicked him into a couple more zombies behind him, ignoring the pain from my ribs as I did so.

"You look a mess," the little girl frowned.

"Thanks," I smiled, as we made it out onto the parade ground.

Kegs and Billy had forced a group of zombies away from us

but as I watched, the two of them collapsed under a mass of attacking dead.

"They are so dead," the girl stated.

"Don't be stupid," Rosie snapped. "They're just creating a divergence."

"Get them to the trucks," I said to Cara, passing the scared little girl to her.

They moved away – I had to push Rosie after them – and I looked around the parade ground. It was a war zone. Kim and a handful of others had made it to the garages only to find the dead heading towards them as well. A couple of Mack's crew (I was already thinking of him rather than Glover as their leader) were already down. They were now using their rifles as clubs (Mack had retrieved his), and had formed a small line to keep the dead at bay, trying to buy more time for those in the garages. Another fell as I watched. I tried to move towards them but suddenly felt amazingly weak. I staggered back, one arm against the nearby wall, the world starting to spin away.

"No time for a nap," Doug said, putting an arm under my shoulder to help me walk.

I was thinking of a snappy comeback when something hit Doug and he went down, blood pouring from his shoulder.

The dead parted and Glover appeared, staggering towards me, less than twelve yards away. A gun in his dead hand.

"I will not die," he growled, in a voice not remotely alive.

I glanced down at Doug. He was still conscious but clearly in pain, blood rushing from his shoulder.

"Do me a favour," he coughed. "Kick his head in."

The window behind me smashed. Glover seemed annoyed at

this. Death was obviously affecting his aim.

The gun went off again. This time I heard the bullet ricochet off the wall behind me.

His aim was getting better.

Glover let out a growl of annoyance as he tried to direct the gun at me once more.

"Alex!" Rosie shouted, rushing back towards me – and straight into the zombies standing by Glover's side. "Bat!"

Rosie hurled her bat above the dead. I dove towards it just as Glover's gun fired, the bullet ricocheting against the wall where I'd been standing a second before. I grabbed the bat and rolled to my feet, using it to smack the gun from Glover's dead hand.

Glover looked at the fallen weapon and then back at me, his dead eyes burning with hatred.

"Can't kill the dead," he hissed.

I brought the bat back towards Glover's face but his hand moved up and grabbed it. He was quicker than the other corpses I'd seen, and stronger. Both of us now held onto the bat, struggling for possession of it. His left hand snaked out to my neck.

"Loser," his dead voice growled.

It was hard to breathe. I could feel the last reserves of energy leaving me as he pushed me back to the wall and lifted me from the ground.

"Get off him," Rosie yelled.

She darted forward, punching Glover's legs.

"I warned you," he snarled, looking down at her, letting go of my neck as he did so.

I collapsed to the ground and looked up as he raised the bat to Rosie. "Now I'll have to kill you."

Desperate, I threw myself at Glover, pushing him backwards into the zombies around him.

"No," I screamed, hitting him again and again. "You won't kill anyone ever again."

"Best you got?" Glover snarled.

"No," I said, grabbing the fallen bat and rising to my feet, allowing Glover to do the same.

His dead face was a mess, bone sticking out of his broken nose, but his eyes still blazed hatred.

"I win," his dead voice mocked.

We didn't move. Everything seemed to pause. Even the zombies around us seemed to hold their corpse-breath.

And then we were rushing towards each other. No words. No threats. We both knew this was the final move. I sidestepped his arm as it swung wildly towards me and brought the bat into his stomach, spinning around and bringing it back up towards his head.

"This one's for Charlie," I said, seconds before the bat hit home.

There was a sound of dead bone smashing and Glover's corpse was lifted off the ground under the impact. He landed on the wet tarmac with a dull thud. This time, he didn't move. For a moment, the zombies stared down at his unmoving corpse and then staggered over him towards myself and Rosie.

"I don't want to die," she sobbed, as I pulled her closer and stepped back to the wall, swinging the bat in front of us in a futile attempt to keep the zombies at bay.

"We're not going to," I lied.

We were surrounded. Too many dead to count. My friends too far away to help.

This is it, I thought. This is where they finally get us.

There was a huge explosion at the gates and corpses could be seen flying into the air, dead a second time.

"Is that thunder?" Rosie asked.

"No," I whispered, a smile crossing my face. "It's the cavalry."

Cadets were rushing into the parade ground. Some on motorbikes, skirting the dead like knights on horseback, using bats to take them down. In the centre of the attack was an armoured truck, Johnny standing on it yelling orders. His father would have been proud.

There were over fifty Cadets with Johnny and two more trucks behind him. Cadets were leaping from them, screaming and shouting as they did so.

And as the dead fell, I saw someone else entering the parade ground. An Alsatian by her side, the dead backing away from the dog's snapping jaws.

"Gabs," I whispered.

"Well, what are we waiting for?" Kim screamed from the garages. "Let's help them!"

With a roar the rest of my friends rushed into the battle.

The zombies were beat. They might not have been outnumbered but they were outfought. Those that didn't collapse started to stagger away from the parade ground, some primeval instinct for survival telling them to leave.

Within a couple of chaotic minutes, the battle was over.

"See," I said, smiling down at Rosie. "Told you we wouldn't die."

"But where's Nigel?" Rosie sniffed, trying not to cry.

It took me a moment to realise she meant Kegs. No one used his real name at school. I looked over to the left, to a pile of unmoving dead near the door where Kegs had made his final stand with Billy.

"I don't think he made it," I started to say, only to see the corpses start to move.

"Geronimo!" Kegs rose from the sea of dead, looking like some kind of Viking berserker, his face bloody and bruised as he dragged a surprised-looking Billy with him.

He glanced around the parade ground, dazed and confused (turns out he'd been unconscious for a while) and then seemed upset when he realised the fight was over. Rosie rushed towards him.

"Nice divergence," she sobbed.

I smiled and was about to say something when I collapsed against the wall.

"I am so sick of almost getting killed," I heard Billy say from nearby.

"Me too," I whispered. "Me too."

I must have passed out for a while, because the next thing I knew Rebel was licking my face and my sister was hugging me.

"Don't ever do that again," she said. "I thought you were dead."

"I don't think your brother's ever going to die," Rosie said. "He's too stubborn."

Gabs laughed at this.

"I thought you were supposed to save me?" she teased.

The rain stopped on cue and I swear the sunset was a brilliant red.

Of course I had concussion so I might have been mistaken about that.

"You must be Gabs," Kim said, sitting next to me on the wet tarmac. Rebel looked at her for a moment and then allowed Kim to fuss her.

"Are we safe now?" a young kid asked, as the Cadets closed the gates to the Centre. Already a couple of the dead were standing there, staring at us.

Waiting.

"Yeah," I said. "We're safe."

"At least for a while," Gabs added.

EIGHTEEN

And that's about it. After all that time trying to get home to save her, it turned out Gabs saved my life.

All of our lives.

Gabs had been as good as her word and managed to find Johnny and the other Cadets. They'd also found reinforcements and were coming back to get Glover and his crew. Not everyone survived, though. Mack was the only one of Glover's gang to make it through the fighting, but his wounds from the zombie attack at my house had been far worse than they appeared. He died a couple of days later. We had a funeral for him. For all of them. We built pyres and sent them off as heroes. I think they'd have liked that.

My gang somehow made it through intact and I'm still not sure how. I spent a couple of days in a makeshift infirmary, with Gabs and Kim fussing over me. Then news came in that a proper rescue station had been set up by some Cadets at an old American Air Force base not far away. I stayed there for a couple of months and life sort of became routine. I learned to drive, ride a motorbike and do first aid. We went on patrol and found kids who'd survived the Change. We heard lots of rumours about what had caused it. The one that came up most was that a drug created to prevent ageing had somehow gone wrong. We even started to hear rumours that the scientist who'd created it was still alive. Kids all over the country are looking for him, but he's yet to be found. Maybe one day he will be.

I never did see my folks again, and I'm glad about that. I like to think they're out there somewhere and one day we will get a cure and they'll be okay again.

That we'll all be okay again.

It's close now. I can feel it. I did wonder what it was like and now I'm going to find out. I feel… strange. I know that's a rubbish description but it's the best I can do. I'm not in pain and I don't feel feverish or anything, I just have a sensation that something is about to happen.

I took the walk a day ago. That's something we started a while back. No one wanted to turn and attack their friends, so when Matt turned eighteen, he told everyone that he wanted to go for a walk.

It was an idea that stuck.

The gang had a birthday party for me a day early. Everyone in the base turned out for it. I looked around, and for a second I could almost see Charlie and the others who didn't make it laughing with us all as they toasted my health and sang "Happy Birthday".

We even had cake!

There was joking and crying – Gabs was taking it bad. That broke my heart. I didn't want to leave her but I had to.

I didn't want to leave any of them.

"Maybe you won't change," Gabs said, but she knew it wasn't true and that I would. Just like she knew, deep down, that I had to leave.

Kegs came up to say goodbye. There were tears in his eyes, and for once he didn't seem to mind.

"You're a good mate," he said. "One of the best."

"Take care of her for me, will you?" I asked Rosie and Chris, who were also crying.

"I promise," Chris said, reaching out and holding Gabs by the hand.

I smiled at that. It made me feel good. I remembered Charlie's funeral then, and Doug's words about who we touch as we live our lives.

I'd been lucky.

I'd had parents who loved me and friends who loved me.

It had been a good life.

Kim gave me one last kiss and I felt like the Star of one of those old westerns my dad used to love – where the hero used to ride off into the sunset.

They opened the gates and I walked out.

I didn't look back.

And here I am.

I'm still writing. That's probably weird, as I've finished my story. I have nothing else to say. It's just that I feel if I keep writing, I'll be fine.

They didn't find Glover's body. Did I mention that? Before we left the TA Centre we cleaned up, but there was no sign of him. I still remember the look of hatred in his eyes and his dead voice as it spoke. He was a zombie, but he knew who he was.

He held on to his humanity, at least some of it.

If Glover could do that then so can I.

Here's a weird thing, as well. Just went to the balcony for one last look at the sunset and now there are loads of dead waiting below. I swear they're waiting for me, but why? Why would they wait for me to change?

Here it comes.

I can feel it now.

Gotta stay in control. Gotta keep writing.

Just worked out who I'm writing this for.

It's not for you.

It's for me.

It's to remind me who I am when I change. I want to remember. I want to live.

I don't want to die.

I remember my dad turning forty and saying you don't enjoy birthdays as much when you get older.

Think he had a point.

This birthday sucks.

I am Alex Stevens and I will not die.

I am Alex Stevens and I will not die.

I am Alex Stevens and

I WILL

NOT

DIE!

ACKNOWLEDGEMENTS

Hope you enjoyed the book. If you did, please leave a quick
review online at Amazon, Good Reads, Kindle or one of
the many other digital book sites popping up. It's a crowded
marketplace and a book needs all the help it can get to reach a
wider audience – and online reviews really do work. I also want
to thank a few people who've helped the creative process. First
and foremost Gary Gilbert for the ace book design, and Lalit
Kumar Sharma and Alan Craddock for the amazing cover art.
More thanks go to Melanie Scott for a much-needed editorial
assist, and to the original readers: John Tomlinson, Glenn Dakin
and Nick Abadzis. Special thanks to Tim Quinn for helping
promote *Zombie 18*.

Lightning Source UK Ltd.
Milton Keynes UK
UKHW040607310319
340211UK00001B/55/P